HEISMAN'S
FIRST TROPHY

100TH ANNIVERSARY

HEISMAN'S
FIRST TROPHY

The Game That Launched Football in the South

GA. TECH. 222
CUMBERLAND·U·0
OCT. 7th. 1916

SAM HATCHER

Published by Franklin Green Publishing
P.O. Box 51
Lebanon, Tennessee 37088
www.franklingreenpublishing.com

Printed in the United States of America

ISBN 9781-936487-332

This is a work of fiction. Critical events in the story took place and individuals who participated are portrayed as may be imagined. Efforts have been made to provide an interesting story that correctly presents critical facts surrounding the game, and the role of the colorful cast of characters who participated in the event.

Cover and Interior Design: Bill Kersey, www.kerseygraphics.com

Edited by Ken Beck

TO FAMILY

I dedicate this book to my wife Teresa; her parents, Frank and Carolyn Dudley; my two sons-in-law, Caleb Dennis and Ryan Sprouse, both graduates of Cumberland; our daughters Kalyn and Karah; and to my parents the late John and Billie Hatcher.

Cumberland University has touched the lives of many in our region although not anywhere close to the thousands who have been educated at Georgia Tech.

Within my own family my wife, mother, sons-in-law, and I are alumni of Cumberland.

The existence of this grand old university founded in 1842 is important to us all and to the community in which we live.

Thank goodness the game about which this book is written was played in 1916 and Cumberland was saved once again.

Resurgam, "I shall rise again."

CONTENTS

FOREWORD

Versions of American football have been recorded as early as 1820 when Princeton students played a mob-like game called "ballown." In that game players were allowed to advance the ball by any means available including their fists, their feet, whatever.

Harvard introduced a version of football in 1827 called "Bloody Monday," which featured freshmen and sophomore classes battling it out in a game that often resulted in riots on campus and in the city of Boston.

In these early days, a couple of decades past the turn of the century, football had a critical need for refining. Some would say taming. Although audiences were fascinated by the game, patrons were beginning to surmise that the sport had no real value other than being a display of blood, violence and unsupervised play.

Rules for football were soon developed. The standards applied to the game ensured competition would be fair, teams would be treated equally, that rules would be consistent and enforced the same from one school to the next, and that the safety of players would be a primary concern.

By the late 1800s many colleges and universities were competing in the sport, rivalries had been developed, and because of a growing fan base so passionate about this relatively new American pastime, the nation's media reacted adding football coverage, including opinion columns, to sports pages inside newspapers.

Each week a new story was being told. There were deaths on the field, hidden ball tricks, the introduction of the forward pass, and the creation of legendary coaches.

Of all the stories told from the beginning of football time in America until today there has not been a more compelling story than the David and Goliath match up in 1916 that pitted the small and obscure Cumberland University in Lebanon, Tenn. against football legend John Heisman and his nationally ranked Georgia Tech Engineers.

It's a romantic memoir that features a gallant and heroic effort of 14 fraternity brothers who volunteered their service to save their small but prestigious university from bankruptcy by playing a football game in Atlanta. And it's the telling first steps for a major university that has developed its football program to become one of the nation's most prominent.

Both universities adopted football programs late in the 19th century. Georgia Tech lost 12–6 in its opening game against Mercer in 1892 and Cumberland two years later tied Peabody College, a Nashville school that later merged with Vanderbilt, 6–6 in its football debut.

Today both Tech and Cumberland continue their respective football traditions albeit Cumberland competes in the NAIA and Tech as a contender in the NCAA Division I.

Beyond football both schools have produced or staked claim to notable alumni, faculty members, or in the case of Georgia Tech, a legendary coach, the late John W. Heisman.

Cumberland University's honor roll of graduates includes a U.S. Secretary of State, more than 80 members of the U.S. Congress, two justices of the U.S. Supreme Court, three U.S. Ambassadors, a number of state governors, scores of state and federal judges, and hundreds of elected local and state officials.

Also graduating from Cumberland was George E. Allen, an advisor to four U.S. presidents and the person primarily responsible for the historic game played between his alma mater and Coach Heisman's Georgia Tech team in Atlanta.

Following Tech's record pounding 222–0 defeat of Cumberland, much has happened in the world. Two World Wars have been fought. The U.S. has recovered from two devastating collapses in its economy. Man has landed and walked on the moon. And the world has experienced many more accomplishments, events, and catastrophes.

Meanwhile college football is alive and well and Georgia Tech and Cumberland, still very different in very many ways, continue to provide the academic discipline in the classroom and orderly prowess on the athletic field to produce quality driven and capable graduates who are determined to make tomorrow's world better for all.

CHAPTER
ONE

FORTY YEARS
AGO TODAY

Getting past Ann to Ike

"The President's office, please.

"Good morning, Ann. It's George. What kind of day does he have today? I'm hoping we might get in eighteen before the rain and some cooler weather comes in later."

Ann Whitman was President Dwight D. Eisenhower's personal secretary. She knew when he could play golf and when he couldn't. A stern woman, whom Eisenhower had met during his campaign for the presidency, Ann could be difficult at times particularly when dealing with an obstinate George Allen.

Ann was no pushover by any measure. Lured from a high-ranking secretarial post with the Crusade for Freedom Organization in New York City at the age of forty-four, she was hired by the Eisenhower campaign team in 1952. After he was elected to America's top office, she was chosen by the president to be his confidant and go-to-person at the White House for the eight years he served.

George and Ann's personalities were often in conflict.

At times they even struggled to understand each other's dialect. George spoke with a deep-southern native Mississippi drawl, while Ann would counter with a sharp and deliberate northern Ohio oral rapid fire.

Nonetheless, George knew how to deal with Ann. And Ann knew she had to tolerate George because he was close to the president and a force with whom to be dealt in Washington political circles.

George commenced his relationship with Eisenhower during the 1940s when he made frequent trips to England and Europe on behalf of the American Red Cross. Their visits developed into a close friendship, and Ann was aware of their history.

Despite their differences Ann and George could find some mutual ground due to their background. George, a dozen years older than Ann, was raised in Baldwyn, Mississippi, a hamlet in the northeast corner of the state only a couple of counties

President Eisenhower

George Allen

removed from Memphis. Ann hailed from Perry, Ohio, a tiny crossroads-like community that bordered Lake Erie.

The two also shared similar sentiments about their college days. Both attended small colleges. Ann's alma mater was Antioch College in Yellow Springs, Ohio, while George graduated from Cumberland University in Lebanon, Tennessee. The two private schools had been founded in the mid-1800s before the Civil War: Cumberland in 1842 and Antioch in 1850.

The one element above all else that connected them most was the absolutely essential need for a close relationship with the president.

Ann wasn't about to give up her role as the White House protocol mistress, and George, for the sake of his livelihood, could not afford a breach with the Oval Office.

The lobbyist, dealmaker, opportunist, and political insider had to get along with "Miss Ann" in order to get along in Washington.

He knew it.

And she knew it.

"He's got a full schedule today. I can't see him getting out of the office. Sorry George, it just doesn't look like there's any possibility of a four-hour opening for a round at Burning Tree. Not today at least," Eisenhower's control officer declared.

He had advised presidents

Before he wound down his career, George Allen would have advised four U.S. Presidents including Roosevelt, Truman, Eisenhower and Kennedy. He had been a key leader in the National Democratic Party, had accepted a number of presidential appointments, many of which were for assignments in foreign countries, and had been at one time in his younger days a pretty damn good courtroom country defense lawyer.

Hearing Ann say "no" didn't come easy for him, especially on this day.

It was Friday, October 7, 1960. Ike was in the midst of a crisis with Russian leader Nikita Khrushchev.

The popular television series *Route 66* would be making its national debut that evening, but taking center stage in the minds of many Americans was the second Kennedy-Nixon debate which

Kennedy-Nixon debate

was to be broadcast by host NBC and carried live as well by CBS and ABC, at 7:30 p.m. Eastern Time.

Sixty million Americans were expected to be sitting in front of their televisions on this night when NBC newsman Frank McGee, the debate moderator, would welcome the audience. Most of the viewers would be watching on sets that provided black-and-white reception only. And many on their way home from work would steal a glimpse of the debate as they passed department store windows where the latest technology in television sets including elaborate wooden consoles would be on display.

George knew that if he and Ike were going to play golf they'd have to be finished before an autumn sun began to disappear and early enough for the president to return to the White House so he could wrap any unfinished business and be ready to watch John F. Kennedy and Richard M. Nixon go at each other for a second time.

The first debate had scored major points for the Kennedy campaign. The attraction for the audience for the second debate, which focused on civil rights, was to see if Nixon could rebound.

George, a former ranking member of the National Democratic Party holding key leadership posts as secretary and treasurer, had a stake in the Kennedy-Nixon race. Although a close friend and confidant of Eisenhower, George was buried in the trenches with the Kennedy campaign. He had bundled thousands of dollars in campaign contributions, worked with key campaign operatives on a number of strategic decisions for the South, and had helped where he could in other parts of the country.

Ike, a Republican, knew George was in the other camp working for Kennedy but respected his position and did not let that come between their friendship or their competitive spirit on the golf course or, for that matter, friendly exchanges over a couple of J.W. Black Labels on the rocks after they left the links.

Pushing a tad more, George insisted to Ann to let him speak to the president.

EISENHOWER'S DRINK OF CHOICE

President Eisenhower, who suffered a number of heart attacks which were largely blamed on his chain-smoking habit, didn't often drink more than one cocktail a day but sometimes would slip and have a couple if he thought word would not get back to his doctor. His favorite libation was J.W. Black Label scotch on the rocks.

Doubtful and resistant as she was, she obliged, warning that the president had but a few minutes to spare.

The Oval Office phone rang a couple of times, and finally the president's voice came over the line. He had been alerted by Ann that George Allen was calling.

Let's do Burning Tree at 11:30

After a quick exchange of greetings, George immediately got down to business.

"Look, I know you've got a full day ahead of you, but I have an 11:30 tee time at Burning Tree. We can easily be finished by 3:30, so you can get back to dealing with that Russian son-of-a-bitch and still have time to watch the debate tonight," George pleaded.

A unique private club, located in Bethesda, Maryland, Burning Tree Golf Club is situated on two-hundred and forty-four extremely well-manicured acres.

"The Tree's" reputation, since it opened in 1923, boils down to really one rule: "no women allowed."

According to history, Burning Tree was conceived after a male foursome at the Chevy Chase Country Club was stuck behind a slow-playing group of female golfers.

Burning Tree has been the club of choice for seven presidents, members of congress, wealthy business executives, high-paid lobbyists, and television celebrities, among others.

The elite who have held memberships at Burning Tree, besides Eisenhower, include Presidents Franklin Roosevelt, John Kennedy, Lyndon Johnson, Richard Nixon, Gerald Ford, and George H. Bush; Supreme Court Chief Justice Warren Burger; print-media mogul William Randolph Hearst; and famed broadcast journalist Edward R. Murrow.

Stories have been told that Tip O'Neill, when he was House Speaker, would play golf at Burning Tree shirtless, which must have proven quite a sight for a man weighing in close to 300 pounds.

A great deal of lore surrounds Burning Tree. Supposedly a helicopter once had to make an emergency landing on the golf course with a U.S. Secretary of State aboard. Two security agents accompanying him were female. All the passengers in the helicopter were allowed to disembark and retreat to the clubhouse except for the two females, who had to stay on the government chopper until appropriate service vehicles came to the club to retrieve the entire group.

House Speaker Tip O'Neil

The club was so beloved by Eisenhower that he maintained a desk and special telephone in the locker room from where he could conduct business between rounds or in between reshuffles of an occasional locker room card game.

Today, in a corner of the downstairs museum-like clubhouse edifice, Eisenhower's massive, white-oak desk and his black, rotary-dial telephone, that during his presidency served as a "hot line" to the White House, command a place of honor.

NO FEMALES

Burning Tree has but one rule: No Females Allowed. Women are provided no facilities whatsoever at the private club. If a taxi cab brings a golfer to the entrance and the driver is female, the passenger/golfer must leave the cab at the gate, wait for a ride to the bag drop, or call for a club attendant to come with a club vehicle and carry him to the clubhouse. Female taxi drivers are not allowed on the grounds.

Although the club has pronounced its prejudice against women, this has not been the case when accepting African-American members. Burning Tree began enlisting black members decades before Augusta National welcomed its first in the 1990s.

For a very long while women were allowed on the grounds of Burning Tree once a year. In December a limited number of weekdays have been set aside for a period of two hours, from 9 o'clock to 11 o'clock, when wives of members may enter the club's pro-shop and purchase Christmas gifts.

The six hundred-member club requires an initiation fee of $75,000 and is open to membership by invitation only.

"OK, OK," the president reluctantly agreed to George's plea. "I might not have time to hit practice balls, but I'll be there by 11:15."

When Ike said he might not have time to hit practice balls, George knew what that meant.

Ike's standard routine for practice was to hit a dozen or so drives from the first tee. Once he hit one long and straight, he'd claim it, and the round would officially begin.

Thrilled at the president's response, George planned the rest of his morning before departing for Burning Tree.

He reached the club just before 10, grabbed a bucket of balls and headed to the practice range a couple of hundred yards from the clubhouse. While he delivered a flurry of shots with his mid-irons and wedge, the painful memory of where he was this day forty-four years ago began to gnaw on his mind.

Patiently waiting for the president, he finished whacking his full bucket of range balls and then spent fifteen minutes on the practice putting green. Even though there was no sign of the president, he ambled to the first tee.

The clock ticked closer toward 11:20. Foursomes were backed up like a minor traffic jam on the Beltway. Nice weather brought them all out thought George, realizing that if Ike didn't get there soon, they'd lose their tee time, no matter if his playing foe for the day was the President of the United States.

Then came the unmistakable roar of the presidential limousine and its accompanying four-vehicle caravan of security agents.

It was Ike, dressed and ready to play.

Dealing with the Russians

"Gosh, I didn't think you were going to make it. What in the hell's going on?" George barked, observing that Ike was somewhat disconnected, a characteristic not often seen in this president, who always came to a golf game with a take-no-prisoner attitude.

KHRUSHCHEV'S VISIT

A 1960 pow wow with Soviet Premier Nikita Khrushchev turned into a testy challenge for President Eisenhower. Nearing the end of his term, he had been in direct conflict with the Soviet leader dating back to an incident on May 1. 1960 in which the Russkies shot down a U-2 spy plane conducting reconnaissance over the U.S.S.R.

In October 1960 Khrushchev made his second visit to the U.S. He had visited in 1959 before the U-2 incident on more agreeable terms when Eisenhower was pushing to have the dividing wall in Berlin removed. However, on this trip the predicament required much more time and finesse.

"It's this raging cold war with the Russians," Eisenhower began.

"I'm starting to believe Patton was right fifteen years ago when he said we ought to go on and take out those bastards (the Soviet Union) at the end of World War II.

"George, I'm telling you that damn Khrushchev is a piece of work. He's coming here next week, and I'm not sure what to expect, but I've got to be prepared for anything," said the frustrated president.

Gen. George Patton brought the Russians into Eisenhower's wheelhouse near the end of World War II when the iconic military hero went on a public campaign advocating that the United States should launch war against the Communist country.

Patton pounded and pounded his message until Eisenhower, Patton's commanding general, was forced to take action that resulted in reassigning the crusty general to an administrative post that for all practical purposes hushed his verbal rhetoric for good.

Ike's mental meanderings about Patton also brushed up some memories that George retained in relationship to Patton's stopover in a small town that held a special place in George's heart.

George told the president about Patton's appearance on the campus of his alma mater during the World War II maneuvers in Middle Tennessee.

Cumberland University, located thirty miles east of Nashville, served as the headquarters of the Second Army for a two-year period during the war, while eight-hundred thousand soldiers trained across Middle Tennessee before being deployed to the battlefields of Europe.

George shared with Ike the tales he had heard about Patton's pearl-handle pistols and how the sound of his boots echoed rhythmically as he stomped through Cumberland's Memorial Hall to

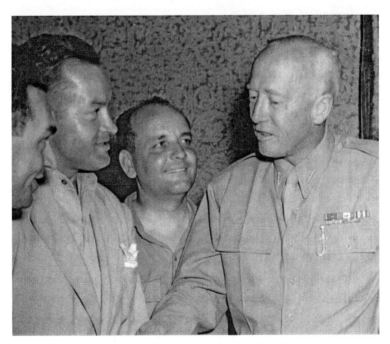

Comedian Bob Hope and George Allen meet with Gen. George Patton

MIDDLE TENNESSEE MANEUVERS

More than twenty Middle Tennessee counties served as a practicing ground for American troops preparing for war in Europe during World War II. For a short time Gen. George Patton's command, the Second Army, claimed Cumberland University as its headquarers.

the commander's office, which previously had been the office of the school president.

While he reminisced, George seemed to be a bit disoriented as his vivid recollections transported him to his college days and specifically to the one day that changed his life.

Taking practice swings

As the duo took a couple of practice swings on the tee, George attracted the concern of his playing partner.

Ike, observing the distant look in George's eyes, was puzzled.

"What the hell is wrong with you?" the president quizzed his pal.

Both men stood braced, resting against their drivers. Henry, one of the older and more experienced African-American caddies at Burning Tree, also noticed the twosome's apparent detachment with respect to today's game.

Henry, who caddied for the pair routinely, knew there was never much money at stake in the round, but bragging rights for the winner proved better than gold.

On a normal day these two would be going at each other like Floyd Patterson and Ingemar Johansson in a world-class heavyweight bout thought the caddy. But today each man was mired in his own world.

Ike, nearing the end of eight years in office, was engulfed with thoughts of what comes next, and he was rankled over the immediate dealings with Khrushchev as well as wrestling with what to do about a vice president who desperately wanted to fill his place in the White House.

George, also nearing the sunset of a successful career in law, business, and national politics, was contemplating his future. Although his thoughts were somewhat more melancholy, as they raced back to a stage set in his life many years ago, and to an event that in some ways defined the course for his future.

George's big day paled in comparison to the Normandy Invasion, the single greatest event in Eisenhower's life.

When Eisenhower gave the orders for D-Day on June 6, 1944, he had no idea the successful invasion that saved the free world would set him up for a tenure in the White House ten years later.

George Allen's day of glory rescued a school from death and prepared him for a life in a world dominated by business and politics.

Remembering relationships

Peering down Burning Tree's first fairway, a stunning, tree-lined almost level 410-yard track, George could see considerable color in the surrounding foliage. Crimson, burnt orange and deep purple hues were framed by a scant collection of surviving green leaves that hung like parachute canopies along the edges of the fairway.

Before they struck their first shots, George began to regale the president about his days as a law student at Cumberland University. Ike knew a bit of George's collegiate days but very little of the details.

The president did have other friends who had graduated from Cumberland. Many of them were lawyers and judges. Some were state governors and quite a few were members of the House or U.S. Senators.

Founded in 1842 in Lebanon, Tennessee, Cumberland University's alumni roll includes fourteen state governors, more than eighty members of Congress, two U.S. Supreme Court Justices, three U.S. Ambassadors, and one Secretary of State Cordell Hull, who served FDR during World War II.

Although Eisenhower knew and shared an intimate relationship with former U.S. Senator and Kansas Governor Arthur Capper, who had graduated from Cumberland's Law School, he knew perhaps better and had an even closer relationship with Secretary Hull, who had been an ally and a mentor to the general during much of the war.

Secretary of State Cordell Hull

Eisenhower gleaned much from Hull, the longest-serving Secretary of State. Appointed to the post by Roosevelt in 1933, he ably filled those responsibilities for nearly 12 years before leaving office in 1944. Hull, who graduated from Cumberland in 1891, was credited with creating the United Nations.

Hull and Eisenhower bonded tightly during the war, as Roosevelt, for the most part, entrusted the responsibility of overseeing the military stateside with Hull, while Eisenhower commanded the war efforts in Europe.

Through this friendship, Ike gained considerable familiarity about Cumberland University. He often asked for advice from Hull, knowing that Hull would apply the wisdom of a rural Tennessee country boy when judging people, whether it be officers under Eisenhower's command, the leaders of enemy

IKE'S CUMBERLAND TIES

Besides Gen. Patton, Secretary Hull and George Allen, President Eisenhower shared a number of other friendships, political alliances, and acquaintances with Cumberland University connections.

The president knew many Cumberland alumni who served in Congress while he was president. In fact, Cumberland, as late as the mid-1970s, was second only to Harvard University as having the most alumni as sitting members of Congress.

One other notable Tennessee connection, although he did not attend Cumberland University, was Sen. Albert Gore, Sr., a Democrat from Carthage, Tennessee, a rural community about 20 miles from the Cumberland campus. Gore and Eisenhower put political differences aside to develop a close friendship, and in 1956 passed legislation creating the nation's interstate highway system.

troops, or, as it had been in more recent years, the Democrats and Republicans ruling Capitol Hill.

Ike's on the first tee

Ike teed off first, rapping the ball two-hundred-and-ten yards down the heart of the fairway.

George waited to see if Ike would hit a second ball, so that he could select the better of the two drives to play. That was Ike's standard operation of procedure on the first tee, and who would argue with him. After all he was the president and leader of the free world.

But today, to George's surprise, Ike decided not to put another ball in play. He would go with his first shot as it was in good shape resting in the fairway.

In a gesture of fair play Ike advised George that he would keep the first drive but would allow George to hit a mulligan if his first shot wasn't acceptable.

Ike, bragging to George about the quality of his tee shot, which had landed squarely in the heart of the fairway and then rolled another 30 yards, attempted to fuel the emotions of the game. When he and George played they were like two kids at a sixth-grade school recess. They continually taunted and badgered one another until the last putt drained into the cup on 18, even keeping up their good-natured needling until sipping their first drink at Burning Tree's 19th-hole bar.

But today was different.

Ike soon forgot his conflict with the Russian leader and put aside his regard for whether or not Nixon would show well in the debate that night against Kennedy.

George, on the other hand, could not escape his past. His mind continued to reel over that fateful day in 1916.

Consternation began to set in with Ike, who was somewhat disappointed that his bantering could not provoke George's wrath as it typically did with the old frat boy who held a vocabulary full of expletives at the tip of his tongue. The president recognized that his golf buddy had his mind on something miles away.

Concerned, Ike gently quizzed his pal how things were going and why his emotions seemed out of sorts.

Fumbling through his pocket in search for a tee, George never looked up nor did he respond.

Pressing harder, the president attempted to persuade George to open up and spill his guts, thinking, perhaps, he could listen and share some sound advice.

ALLEN MEETS EISEHHOWER

George Allen met Dwight Eisenhower when he was making trips to Europe in the 1940s as a representative of the Red Cross. He accepted a presidential appointment as a director of the War Damage Corporation, a government agency created as the result of World War II to provide insurance against war-related damages to private property held by Americans. In 1944, he served President Harry Truman as campaign manager when Truman was on the ticket as a vice presidential candidate.

In 1946 Allen became director of the Reconstruction Finance Corporation and later that year was featured on the cover of Time Magazine. Despite a close relationship with Eisenhower, a Republican, Allen held key leadership posts in the National Democratic Party. For several years he was a major power broker in Washington because of the relationships he held not only with presidents but with members of Congress and the judiciary.

Still silent, George took two practice swings, addressed the ball and stopped. He looked back over his shoulder to see Ike glaring at him in what appeared to be a stare-down.

George knew he owed the president an explanation.

He paused, turned his attention back to the tiny white ball in front of him and swung as hard as he could. Never watching the flight of the ball, he turned to his friend and began, "Well, I tell you, Ike. It was a day very much like this."

CHAPTER
TWO

NOT COACH HEISMAN'S FIRST RUMBLE WITH CUMBERLAND

Cumberland abandons once prominent football program

From one hole to the next, between drives, chips and putts, George described in intimate detail the historic football game that was played by one team to save its school from bankruptcy and by the other to preserve what it believed to be its pathway to a national collegiate football championship (and its coach's personal vendetta).

On October 7, 1916, tiny Cumberland University played John Heisman's top-ranked Georgia Tech Yellow Jackets in Atlanta, Georgia, in what the sports media of the twenty-first century would have dubbed as "a must game" for each school.

George Allen, a law school student from Mississippi, was recognized at Cumberland as the big man on campus.

His Kappa Sigma fraternity looked to him for leadership as did the student body and, often, school administration officials.

If there was ever a most likely-to-succeed candidate who could not fail from the group of swell fellows at Cumberland, who enjoyed the frat parties and moot court appearances much more than the rigors and complications of studying contract law, George Allen was your man.

KAPPA SIGMA

Founded in 1400 at the University of Bologna, the fraternity was introduced in the United States in 1869 by five students at the University of Virginia in Charlottesville, Va. Kappa Sigma was chartered at Cumberland University in 1887 and at Georgia Tech in 1895.

He was the guy others sought to get them matched with a luscious coed, especially if the event might be a Saturday night party at Horn Springs, a favorite resort about six miles west of campus complete with a swimming pool, train stop, live bands in season, a dance floor and other recreational amenities. George also could clue younger law scholars as to what might be expected on Judge Nathan Green's final examination.

Respected for his quick wit and intellectual capabilities, he was also prized by the administration and faculty. He offered a sound voice from the student side of things when decisions were being discussed that impacted campus life.

In 1916 Homer Allin Hill wore the cloak of Cumberland University president. He had filled the role abducted by Samuel Andrew Coile, who served an abbreviated term from 1914 to 1916.

These were trying times at Cumberland, as Hill wrestled with a major issue from behind his desk in the president's office.

Cumberland had been identified in some academic circles as "the Harvard of the South."

It had faced previous challenges, none bigger, than during the Civil War when on August, 29, 1864, Union troops torched the main building on the university's original campus less than a mile east of the present campus along West Spring Street.

The original administration building housed the art, law and theology schools. The magnificent structure had been designed by renowned architect William Strickland, who also planned the Tennessee State Capitol and many other fine edifices across the South as well as signature works in Philadelphia and other cities in the Northeast.

Mounting financial issues were threatening to shutter the school in the spring of 1916, thus President Hill and board members came to the conclusion that Cumberland's flailing football program must be shuttered.

It was not a decision made in haste but only after careful deliberation. The University's leadership had decided there was but one option: it was fourth down and long and time to punt.

George and his peers were in an uproar about the school's decision to disband the sport. After all, football had once been almost as important to the University as its nationally prominent law school.

In previous seasons leading up to this reckoning Cumberland teams had played national powerhouses such as Mississippi, Alabama, Tulane, Vanderbilt, South Carolina, Louisiana State, Tennessee, Georgia Tech and Clemson, among others.

The 1903 Cumberland football team claimed the Southern Conference championship after beating Tulane, LSU and Alabama over a five-day span and then tying Clemson in a postseason game arranged by Clemson coach John Heisman.

By 1916 Cumberland had posted a notable list of who's who in college football ranks. To abort the gridiron program likely would send a strong message across the South that this exalted bastion of higher education was on the cusp of extinction.

John Heisman standing on Bowman Field, in front of Tillman Hall, on the Clemson University Campus.

Unlike contemporary college athletic programs where games are contracted as much as five years in advance, the plotting of schedules was not so disciplined during this era. Schools often added or dropped adversaries as the season approached, and on occasion would even drop a game while the season was in progress.

It was not uncommon for a school to play two consecutive weekends, skip a couple of weeks, and then resume their

MAJOR SOUTHERN CONFERENCE

Established in 1894, the Southern Intercollegiate Athletic Association, (SIAA) was one of the earliest college athletic conferences.

At its height the organization had seventy-two members covering the Southeastern U.S. It dissolved in 1942.

Membership included all current schools in the Southeastern Conference with the exceptions of Arkansas, Missouri and Texas A&M. Also in its ranks were twelve current members of the Atlantic Coast Conference and the University of Texas.

Vanderbilt chemistry professor Dr. William Dudley founded the conference with luring Alabama, Auburn, Georgia, Georgia Tech, North Carolina, Sewanee and Vanderbilt as charter members.

Clemson, Cumberland University, Kentucky, LSU, Mercer, Mississippi, Mississippi State, Southwestern Presbyterian, Tennessee, Texas, Tulane, and the University of Nashville enlisted in 1895.

The conference mission statement announced it was created for "the development and purification of college athletics throughout the South."

Among other member schools in later years were Centenary, Centre, Chattanooga, The Citadel, Dahlonega (North Georgia), Davidson, Delta State, Eastern Kentucky, Emory and Henry, Erskine, Florida,

Continued

33

Furman, Georgetown (Kentucky), Gordon Military College, Howard College (Samford), Jacksonville State (Alabama), Kentucky Wesleyan, Louisiana College, Louisiana Tech, Louisville, Loyola (New Orleans), Memphis State, Memphis University School, Miami, Middle Tennessee, Millsaps College, Morehead State (Kentucky), Newberry, Northwestern State (Louisiana), Oglethorpe, Presbyterian (South Carolina), Rollins, Southern (Florida), Southern Mississippi, Southern University (Alabama), Southwestern Presbyterian (Rhodes, Memphis), Southwestern Louisiana, Spring Hill (Alabama), Stetson, Tampa, Tennessee Tech, Transylvania (Kentucky), Trinity College (Duke), Troy State, Tulane, Union (Kentucky), Western Kentucky, and Wofford.

schedule for another six weeks or so. Games might also be slated on consecutive days because of the limitations placed on travel.

Traveling from one city to another was not always convenient. If a team had a road trip in south Alabama for example, it might schedule a game against the University of Alabama in Tuscaloosa on Friday and play Auburn Saturday before returning home.

A team's football season during this era might include as few as six games and as many as eight or nine.

George gets called in

Before the university announced its plans and acknowledged a forecast that would surely create a tsunami-sized negative reaction among students, President Hill called George into his office and articulated why Cumberland's football program was about to be drop-kicked into the dustbin of history.

Hill reasoned that Cumberland teams had not been competitive in recent years and that the school didn't have a sufficient

recruiting plan to attract good players. The University needed
to focus on academics and the law school and not extra-curric-
ular affairs. Finally and of most importance, football was being
quashed because the school was financially strapped and needed
every cent possible to continue operations.

Cumberland, unlike its Ivy League rivals and area state
schools, had never had a substantial endowment or other financial reservoirs from which to draw. For the most part Cumberland
relied on student tuition to pay its bills.

George listened carefully as Hill defended the school's
decision and accepted the outcome without favor but with
understanding.

His role now, in the sight of administration, was to serve as
messenger and mediator to the student body. The administration
would make the announcement but was leaning heavily upon
George's skill to keep the peace with his peers.

Mulling over how best to break such negative news, George
had ideas.

First, he could state the decision made to dismiss the football
program was made solely in the best interest of Cumberland's
students. To keep the University's academics intact, sacrifices had
to be made.

Second, George would deploy a diversionary tactic by telling
his classmates, "We still have baseball, and Saturday we're going
to whip the heck out of Georgia Tech's rambling wreck."

Little did the young law school student realize, but he was
taking the first step to wake up a sleeping giant.

Working his classmates and fraternity brothers into a frenzy
for a baseball game against Georgia Tech seemed like a good
strategy for the moment, but who knew what lay ahead come fall.

From one dormitory to another and at each frat house and
sorority gathering, George made ballyhoo over the upcoming
"whupping" he had planned for Georgia Tech on the baseball
diamond.

A pep rally was slated for Thursday, followed by a "get ready for the big game" party on Friday night at Horn Springs.

The Cumberland baseball schedule in the spring of 1916 featured the likes of Alabama, Vanderbilt, Sewanee, Kentucky, Maryville, Middle Tennessee State, and a couple of games with a few Nashville semi-pro teams.

An excerpt from the school yearbook described Cumberland's baseball team as "very promising."

The annual read: "Overlooking the loss of Turner and Collins to Jersey City, Cumberland still has a chance to win the honor she has always won in the game. On the mound are Bohanon, Thweatt, Estes and Bradshaw, any of who can meet and beat any college team on our schedule."

Drinking George's Kool-Aid

Among his multiple roles on campus, George served as the baseball team's student manager, a job that in these times was similar to that of athletic directors in later decades.

That meant he did it all including scheduling the games. He was so adept at what he did that the only thing baseball coach Peck Turner had to do was make out the lineup and coach his team.

All the hoopla George had stirred on campus about the weekend game against Tech was beginning to take the shape of a seventh game in the World Series. It was purely coincidental that the opposing nine played for Georgia Tech.

Come Friday, P.T. Barnum himself could not have done a more glorious job than George in creating what was now a circus-like environment among students and townspeople. The game had become the talk of the town, especially around the square.

Inside the Devil's Elbow, a sudsy beer-drinking haven for Cumberland students in the northwest corner of Lebanon's Public Square, bets were being made. The odds weren't about whether or not Cumberland would win the game but rather about how badly the Bulldogs would beat Tech.

A number of stores were announcing that they would close early Saturday as they anticipated there wouldn't be many customers with so many folks headed to the game, including many of the merchants themselves and their employees.

Signs encouraging the Cumberland team were posted in store windows, while posters were nailed to utility poles and stapled on tobacco sticks planted in front yards.

Saturday was going to be a day to beat the band, and George was beginning to feel the pressure.

Cumberland's got to win this game he told to himself. "If we don't, I'm the guy they're going to come looking for," he muttered beneath his breath.

Hmm, thought George, "What I need is some sort of insurance policy. Better yet a guarantee."

A rascally smile crossed his face, and George began to walk rapidly to the wooden garage that housed his 1913 Chevrolet Series C Classic Six auto. It was time for a quick solo trip into Nashville.

1913 Chevy

He couldn't afford to be gone long or he would be missed, and he couldn't take a passenger as he was on a top-secret mission of graveyard magnitude and didn't need any witnesses.

By noon, George was pounding the sidewalks of Nashville, visiting saloons where he knew he could find some of the city's best semi-professional baseball players, men who, under the right circumstances, might be willing to commit to a Saturday afternoon of competitive baseball in Lebanon.

His prowess to seek and find was an attribute he claimed from his DNA. George's father was a noted scout for Confederate General Nathan Bedford Forrest during the Civil War.

Within two hours he had signed on three hitters with better than .350 batting averages, a pitcher with the reputation of hurling unhittable fast balls and two flawless-fielding middle infielders.

What would be their payola for one day of baseball in a Cumberland uniform?

The manager promised a lively Friday night party at Horn Springs, a bevy of gorgeous coeds, all the beer they could drink, travel expenses, and, best of all, the opportunity to beat one of the nation's greatest coaches, John Heisman, and his nationally-ranked Georgia Tech Yellow Jackets.

The rapid sale, one of George's fortes, proved simple. The professionals were eager to follow him back to Lebanon for an all-night soiree beside the magical springs. And George had his insurance to cover his baseball diamond. It was a solid package deal, one good for all parties concerned.

In the early years of the twentieth century, the college athletics rulebook was loosie-goosie at best. Teams were allowed to add

HORN SPRINGS RESORT

Founded in 1870, Horn Springs was a popular resort near Lebanon. Its reputation sprouted after the Horn family discovered a spring on the property that provided a special mineral water reported to cure a variety of ills. The water was bottled and sold, while guests could also soak in special baths offered at the spring spa. Besides a hotel, the facilities included a restaurant, dance hall and outdoor entertainment options. Tourists from across the South frequented Horn Springs, often arriving by passenger rail service.

players at the drop of a pop-up fly ball as college baseball was treated more or less like a backyard pick-up game. While adding professional players to the lineup may have been viewed as taking it a step too far, it wasn't anything that hadn't been done by numerous other schools.

Back on campus, George could take a deep breath and relax. He reported to Coach Turner that he had recruited a few extra players for the big game and counseled that they needed to be in the starting lineup if he wanted to have any sort of chance to beat Heisman's superior Tech team.

Saturday morning showed the beginning of a gorgeous spring day. Temperatures were expected to hit the mid-70s by game time.

Fans of the great American pastime began gathering a full hour before the first pitch. Women toted picnic baskets brimming with good eats. Small children dove into playing games in the dirt behind the bleachers, while townsfolk and hundreds of Cumberland students filled the wooden bleachers.

Horn Springs was a popular weekend resort during the early 1900s near Lebanon, Tennessee

Meanwhile, Georgia Tech coach John Heisman, already a legend in the minds of many a sportswriter, readied his squad for the contest and cast a careful eye toward the Cumberland players. This was not his first rumble with Cumberland.

Thirteen years earlier, when he was head coach of the Clemson football team, Heisman met Cumberland on Thanksgiving Day in the inaugural Southern Conference championship game in Montgomery, Alabama.

Both schools had managed winning records during the regular season that ended a couple of weeks earlier. Playing against ranked teams, the two were recognized by sports columnists and national sports publications as two of the nation's top football teams.

Going into the November 26 championship game, Clemson boasted a 4–1 record with victories over Georgia, North Carolina A&M, and Davidson. Their solitary loss was an 11–6 decision against North Carolina.

Cumberland also held a 4–1 record with impressive wins over Vanderbilt, Alabama, LSU and Tulane. Regarded as one of Cumberland's best teams ever, the Bulldogs had outscored opponents in the four wins by a combined 119–0. Their only loss, a 6–0 defeat, came at the hands of the University of the South at Sewanee.

While the two teams played to an 11–11 tie on this late November day, Heisman got a bird's-eye view of this small Tennessee school's tenacity and acumen on the playing field. Cumberland outplayed Clemson in the first half, scoring 11 points and keeping the Tigers scoreless.

Clemson came back in the second half, matching the score with 11 points, and the game ended tied in a knot. So both teams shared the coveted Southern Championship title.

It was the final game Heisman captained at Clemson. But it would not be his last football game to coach against Cumberland, and he did not like the idea of sharing a title.

CHAPTER
THREE

HEISMAN DETECTS CUMBERLAND RINGERS

Batter-up

It was time to play ball.

George, in his role as baseball team manager, had done all that he could to ensure a victory. Winning the game at this point was in the hands of Coach Turner, the semi-pro players from Nashville, and the legitimate Cumberland players who had done quite well for themselves during the earlier part of the season.

The home team fans and students wanted to beat Heisman because of his notoriety and the acclaim he had received from the national press. It was turning out to be more of a case of Cumberland seeking to beat the man behind the team, Coach Heisman, rather than simply beating Georgia Tech.

Heisman had already made his mark as a coach by boasting winning records in two sports at Buchtel and Clemson before arriving at Tech. A household name, the coach was considered the best of the best.

Before he concluded his career, Heisman would mastermind football teams at eight schools including Oberlin College, Buchtel College (now University of Akron), Auburn, Clemson, Georgia Tech, University of Pennsylvania, Washington and Jefferson College, and Rice. As a head football coach for thirty-five years, from 1892 to 1927 he compiled a record of 186 wins, 70 defeats, and 18 ties.

His winning slate in baseball proved equally impressive at 219–119–7.

Off to another strong start with his Yellow Jackets baseball team, Heisman knew a win over a solid Cumberland team would bolster Tech's ranking in the national polls. He yearned to win this match as fervently as George Allen and the Cumberland crowd.

Heisman's expectations in everything he did was to be the best. Whether it be football, basketball (he coached Tech's basketball team for two years), or baseball, he wanted to be Number One.

Winning may not have meant everything, but Heisman had a difficult time explaining to his players how anything could be gained by losing.

He reminded his players frequently of that fact and that they must do their job and stay focused and disciplined at all times.

Coach Heisman admonished the Tech squads he coached, "Gentlemen, it is better to have died as a small boy than to fumble this football."

It was his way of driving home the point to not make unforced errors. He looked upon mistakes made on the football field as a case of players simply not thinking, thus among the gravest of errors in his eyes.

He would not tolerate a lack of focus, minimal effort, or any other personal failure on the part of an individual player that contributed to a loss.

That's why on this day he was shocked.

Georgia Tech was shut out.

Meanwhile, the Cumberland Bulldogs were on fire.

A myriad of more than three dozen hits including a half-dozen home runs sealed the win.

After nine innings Cumberland had demolished Heisman's nationally-ranked Tech team by a score of twenty-two to nothing.

The legendary coach was embarrassed at his team's sound defeat, and he wanted an explanation.

Heisman begins his probe

Coach Heisman gathered his players before for the long trip back to Atlanta. He was still trying to understand how such a defeat could have been thrust upon his talented Georgia Tech team.

As he began to ask about some of Cumberland's star players of the game, he soon realized he had been duped. Cumberland and their handful of ringers had taken his boys to the woodshed for a shellacking

43

Heisman was furious. He knew Cumberland's tactics were not honorable, nonetheless, the record book showed the result as a loss for Tech. George Allen's shenanigans potentially could cost John Heisman a national championship in baseball.

As he turned to leave the playing field, Coach Heisman threw a final glance across the diamond with but one emotion branded in his mind: revenge.

But at this time he could not imagine where he would get the opportunity.

Cumberland and Tech could meet in a baseball game somewhere down the road, but it was not likely. And there was no chance his football squad would collide with the lowly Bulldogs, now one of the weakest teams in the South.

After the game

George hung around the field after the big win. He paid the promised travel expenses to the semi-pro players, congratulated Coach Turner and the real Cumberland players, and shook hands with folks in the crowd as he received countless pats on the back while mingling with the crowd that didn't want the happy mood come to an end.

And for good reason.

The hometown school had handed John Heisman and Georgia Tech the worst defeat that he and Tech had ever experienced on a baseball diamond.

Many newspapers across America carried the story over the following days. Some held forty-eight point headlines proclaiming how Cumberland had man handled the highly-ranked Engineers. Sports columnists speculated on what could have happened in Lebanon to permit such a defeat, as the Tech team dropped from the list of top baseball teams in the nation.

While Heisman held not a clue as to how he would get even, he knew that somehow, some day he would get payback. Seething after the game, he did not refrain in letting Cumberland officials, coaches and others know how he felt, especially George Allen.

George viewed the great man's threats and emotions as hollow. After all what could this coaching icon do to harm Cumberland University? The game was in the books and that was the end of it.

A few days later

Life on campus returned to normal after the weekend of celebrated match.

There wasn't much activity on Sunday because of Blue Laws, which meant restaurants, businesses, especially saloons and taverns, and even the moving picture theater on the public square were closed. The most excitement took place inside local churches after the final prayer as parishioners whispered across the pews about the big game.

On Monday when businesses sprang back to life, the conversation continued in stores, lawyers' offices, the courthouse and

George Allen (seated at far right) on yacht with President Truman

around the square. Chatter drifted from the coverage of the game in the Sunday *Nashville Tennessean* to whether or not Tech might fire Heisman for being on the wrong side of such a one-sided game.

And while Cumberland's Coach Turner received a considerable amount of credit for the win, George was the man of the hour, a big man on and off campus.

Most of the students knew George was the mastermind who crafted the strategy to field a team capable of beating Tech. Ah, but to do so in such an unforgettable fashion, now that was impressive. He had staged the event like a New York City impresario might present a fine theatrical play on Broadway.

A revived spirit abounded on the school campus. A renewed pride in Cumberland thrived throughout the remainder of spring until graduation day when seniors marched and undergraduates returned to their hometowns for the summer break.

With final examinations week approaching, George took a final stab at changing the administration's mind about dropping football. His words proved futile.

The law student had five classes in which he faced extremely challenging final exams. He had no time for frivolous activities at Horn Springs, a night out with a favorite co-ed, or an afternoon of downing beer at the Devil's Elbow on the square.

Winding down his first year of law school, George had to buckle down and take care of why he came to Cumberland in the first place.

Cracking the books didn't come easy for him. It wasn't because of his intelligence but rather because of his choice of being involved in so many activities on campus.

He practically ran Cumberland's athletic department as baseball, basketball and football team manager. He headed the Kappa Sigma fraternity. And he spent a great deal of his free time practicing his budding skill as a raconteur, a talent that would lead him into relationships with four American presidents, numerous leaders of the British Parliament, movie stars, and other notable men and women. His life in the spotlight also landed him numerous appearances in some of the nation's largest newspapers and nationally recognized magazines.

Featured on the cover of *Time* magazine on August 12, 1946, George entertained the publication's readership with stories about his life since childhood including the Cumberland vs. Georgia Tech debacle and a humorous account of his first case as a full fledge attorney in Mississippi.

According to the *Time* story, his client was a lady who had fallen over her umbrella and injured herself at a rail station.

In the account George says on her behalf he sued the railroad for $40,000 and settled for $10. "She got $5 and I got $5," he concludes with a chuckle adding "I was in no mood to dicker."

Mature for his twenty years of age, George was light years ahead of his peers. Before he turned the age of thirty, he would hold key political and business leadership positions that would take him to international prominence.

But this week his focus turned to his law classes, specifically the study of contracts, torts, criminal law, evidence, and domestic relations.

After completing his exams, George had a few final chores to finish before he would make the arduous twelve-hour drive home to Baldwyn. His plans for the summer included working in a family friend's law office in nearby Booneville, Mississippi. There he would have the opportunity to see and practice for real what he had been experiencing in Judge Green's classroom.

Ramping down football

One of his last assignments before departing the campus was to bring final closure to his beloved football team. George had been instructed by university officials to clean out locker rooms, get rid of the football equipment, and do whatever else necessary to ring the death knell on Cumberland's football program.

School administrators thought it best to handle these matters after students had left for the summer. George agreed. Once he had said his final good-byes, he went to work. In two days he was done with the dirty work and reported to President Hill that he had completed his task.

Among his duties related to shuttering the football program was that of notifying schools on next fall's schedule that Cumberland would not be fielding a team. Thus, he wearily wrote letters to the colleges, alerting them of the predicament. He then left for Mississippi, ready for the summer break and already anticipating his return to campus.

But there was one letter he failed to write.

Driving home

George left campus a little before two o'clock in the afternoon. He wouldn't reach Baldwyn until several hours past midnight.

The marathon drive home presented him ample time to digest the end of the school year, whether he had missed a case problem question on divorce on his domestic relations final, and if he'd locked the frat house and completed the work assigned him by the administration with respect to closing down the football program.

Getting to Baldwyn, a two-hundred-and-twenty-five-mile winding excursion from Lebanon was no simple matter. George would drive to the western edge of Nashville and take Highway 100 south to Linden. From there he would motor along state route 128 to Clifton and on to Savannah. From Savannah he would meander along back roads that curved back and forth between Tennessee and Mississippi until he arrived in Corinth. From Corinth, Baldwyn was a straight thirty-two-mile shot.

Along the route, he knew every barbecue smokehouse, beer joint, and off-the-road bootlegger where one could purchase Tennessee or Mississippi moonshine or corn liquor.

George looked forward to getting home and applying some of what he'd learned in the classroom to work in a small-town law office that took on cases that ranged from defending a twelve-year-old youth accused of stealing a couple of apples from a general store to a black man indicted for flirting with a prominent white woman.

A short summer

This summer, between stints in the law office, most often on the weekends, George would explore some of the region's large cotton farms. He had always been fascinated by agriculture.

His interest in husbandry proved a helpful factor in growing his friendship with Eisenhower, who been raised in the midst of the cornfields of Kansas in a poor Mennonite family that raised everything they ate.

Most of the summer George labored in the law office Monday through Thursday, but the other three days he spent on a large cotton farm.

By August he was anxious to get back to his more glamorous life on campus. His earnings for the summer would be applied to tuition, books, board, Kappa Sig dues and, of course, making a portion of his budget for an ample social life.

By Labor Day his bags were packed and the Chevy loaded. He was on the road again, motoring toward Lebanon and Cumberland University.

Never in his wildest dreams could he imagine the turmoil and excitement the fall term would lay squarely at his feet.

CHAPTER
FOUR

BANKRUPTCY LOOMS

Back at Cumberland

"I'm back," George shouted as he entered the frat house front door and threw the first of a collection of suitcases, boxes, and bags on the entrance foyer floor.

Two of his Kappa Sigma brothers had beat him to campus for the fall semester.

George gave his best buddy, Gentry Dugat, a bear hug before darting to the ice box for a bottle of beer.

"So, how was your summer?" asked George as he stretched out on a worn couch and sipped his brew.

Gentry had migrated to Cumberland from Beeville, Texas, a small town about forty miles from Corpus Christi and about a thousand miles from Lebanon.

Gentry would be the first recruit George would nab when he began to fill a roster of volunteers for the battle against the gridiron giant in Atlanta.

CUMBERLAND'S LAW SCHOOL

Cumberland University attracted a number of students from Texas, Oklahoma, Arkansas, and other states west of the Mississippi during the early 20th century. Its reputation made it a school of choice for young scholars wanting to pursue the study of law. Viewed by many as an equal to Harvard, students who lived in the Southwest found it far more convenient than making the trek to Boston.

Among those was T. Boone Pickens, Sr., father of the billionaire oil tycoon, who came from Oklahoma to study law at Cumberland in 1921.

Stepping into the room from an adjoining bedroom came another fraternity brother and bosom pal, Morris Gouger.

Morris had ridden back to school with Gentry. Morris claimed Robstown, Texas, as his home. Located in the extreme southeast part of the state, about one-hundred and thirty miles from San Antonio and just over one thousand miles from Cumberland, Robstown boasted a population of four thousand souls.

Morris snatched a bottle of beer from the ice box and sat down with Gentry and George, and the trio recapped their summer highlights. They discussed the work they did, the girls they swooned, and talked excitedly about the upcoming school year.

Presidential visit

The reunion was interrupted by a knock on the front door of the fraternity house.

George arose from the couch and peered through the screen door to see Cumberland president Homer Hill standing on the front porch. He wore a three-piece suit that surrounded a white heavily starched shirt with tab collar and a subdued striped neck tie.

It was one of those early September days in Middle Tennessee that more resembled the middle of July. The thermometer on the wall, advertising a local funeral parlor, read ninety-six degrees. The humidity was overwhelming, thus Hill sweated profusely as he stood and waited for one of the boys to come to the door.

It was a rare event for the school president to drop by a fraternity house, and typically the cause was not advantageous to those occupying the premises. The last time a top school official paid their respects to the frat house was on an early Monday morning to chew the lads out about a weekend of partying that had run amuck and disturbed residents on neighboring West Spring.

George's mind raced ninety miles an hour, and his pulse zipped to one hundred. He and his buddies scrambled to hide

53

their bottles as they cleared a path so the president could walk inside. George knew this was no social visit.

"Let's go, boys. Open the door," Hill pleaded.

Making a quick sweep of the room and making a few final adjustments, the three were as prepared as they could be in two minutes.

Gentry went to the door and greeted the president.

"President Hill, what a great surprise," he exclaimed as if he didn't know who had been knocking.

"Please come into our humble abode," he offered.

Hill entered and his eyes darted about the room. The three stood nervously with their hands stuffed in their pockets and prayed silently that he would not get a whiff of the beer on their breath.

In a corner, not fully concealed behind a floor lamp, a beer bottle rested horizontally on its side. It had been there for some time, likely all summer. It had been overlooked in the frantic house cleansing only minutes earlier.

Hill spied the bottle, frowned and said sternly, "George, would you come with me? We need to talk."

George thought, "Oh, crap. I haven't even been back an hour and now I'm being called on the carpet by the president but what in the hell for."

The boys recognized that President Hill's demeanor seemed worried. They knew he was a man who abhorred alcohol and constantly preached its evils, so it was telling that he did not scold them over the discovered empty bottle.

They begin to walk

George and the president strolled across the front lawn and stopped beneath a giant oak tree that offered some shade from the hot afternoon sun but little relief from the humidity. They were far enough away from the frat house that they could speak in private.

Hill immediately directed his comments to the heart of the matter.

"George, when you canceled the football games that were set for this fall, did you contact all of the schools?" he asked.

"Yes sir. I'm pretty sure I got in touch with each one," responded the young man in a somewhat shaky voice.

"George, this is of immense importance. I want you to think carefully. Are you positive that you mailed cancellation letters to each school?" the president pressed.

Puzzled by Hill's query, George's confidence began to wane as he reflected on whether he had, indeed, written every college and alerted them that Cumberland would not be fielding a football team this fall and was canceling its entire schedule.

"President Hill, I get the impression that there may be a problem. Am I right?" George asked.

"I'm not sure," Hill said, but "I've received a letter from Georgia Tech stating that they understand from conversations with other universities that Cumberland is not playing football this season and has dropped the sport from its athletic program.

"According to the letter, Georgia Tech never received notice that we were canceling our game with them in October," President Hill explained.

Looking for a quick solution, George told Hill that he would get a missive off to Georgia Tech the next day with the appropriate notice about the situation.

"That may or may not do the trick, George, but from what I gather they're awfully upset and where this goes from here I have no idea," said Hill.

"Go ahead and get letters in the mail first thing in the morning to the president of Georgia Tech as well as to their football coach, John Heisman. Let them know that we inadvertently failed to give them proper notice of our decision to suspend the 1916 season. Tell them that we genuinely regret this oversight and that you, the one responsible for arranging the schedule, and myself, the president of the school, offer our most sincere apologies."

Hill then informed George that in the same letter he received from Tech, there was reference to a contract the two schools had signed for a game to be played October 7, 1916, in Atlanta.

"If they plan to enforce this contract, we may be in hot water. We must get this resolved," the president concluded.

George knew perfectly the mission that had been laid before him. He had to write a convincing communiqué claiming total responsibility for the foul up. His letter must express how remorseful he and President Hill were about the matter, and it had to be worded in such a way as to remove the slightest doubt of any impropriety.

Assuring the president he was up to the task, George walked slowly back to the frat house.

His first night back on campus would prove to be a long one. Putting the premium words on paper would be as difficult a challenge as any of the complex legal issues he studied in the classrooms of his rigid law professors.

Giving it their best shot

By two a.m. the next morning, George found the words coming agonizingly slow. He found it nearly impossible to pen an acceptable apology for what was an honest mistake.

At five o'clock he dueled with himself over the closing paragraph. It had to be spot on as it would serve as the final touch on how to best state "We're sorry."

Dotting the final "I" at seven a.m., George rushed to take a shower, shave and dress, and then sprinted to the president's office where Hill was waiting. He had been there since five o'clock.

George handed over his letter.

Hill slowly read it to himself, then reread it aloud. He pondered each word and studied how every phrase might be interpreted. He tried to put himself in the shoes of those for whom the letter was intended.

After the longest ten minutes of his life, George heard Hill say, "I think this is excellent. This is our best shot. We've got to hope and pray that it will be sufficient."

With that shot of verbal adrenalin, George recused himself from Hill's office and walked as fast as he could for the Lebanon Post Office. He deposited the letter and trudged back to campus. Now all he could do was wait. It would probably be a week before the plea arrived in the hands of the Georgia Tech president Kenneth G. Matheson and Coach Heisman.

George thought it might take two to three weeks before they heard back from Tech.

Not good news

To George and President Hill's surprise it was less than a week before Tech responded. It was not an answer to their prayers. Their best shot, a long shot, had not hit the target.

From Coach Heisman came the words that Cumberland University must play the game as scheduled or pay a fine of three thousand dollars for breach of contract.

That three thousand dollar penalty in 1916 would be the equal of about $100,000 today. The loss would be a devastating blow to Cumberland's stressed financial state.

Hill sent word via a student messenger from his office for George to report to him pronto. The note was succinct. It read: "George, as soon as you are out of class, report to my office."

George was stuck in a class with fifty law students as two of his peers argued a moot court case. An hour remained before all would be finished, and Judge Green, 89, the professor and dean of the law school, was adamant about attendance. He would not tolerate a student missing a day of moot court, and he certainly would not allow an early leave before a session ended.

CARUTHERS HALL

The Cumberland Law School was housed in Caruthers Hall on West Main Street in Lebanon until the early 1960s when the school was sold to Samford University in Birmingham, Alabama. Commonly recognized by students and townspeople as the "Law Barn," the structure closely resembled Philadelphia's

Cumberland's Caruthers Hall,
the "Law Barn"

Independence Hall. Funds for the building, erected in 1878, were contributed by Cumberland's first president, Robert L. Caruthers, a governor of Tennessee for the Confederacy, justice of the state Supreme Court, and member of the U.S. House of Representatives.

The class took place in what was commonly referred to as the Cumberland "Law Barn" on West Main Street. George sat pretending to be engaged but in truth his mind was some five blocks away at the main campus wondering what news President Hill held.

Judge Green adjourned class at noon. George sprinted for Memorial Hall on the main campus, and once inside slowed to a quick walk down the long hall to the president's office.

Since the door was open, George entered and shuffled slowly toward Hill's desk.

"Come on in, George. I'm afraid I've got some bad news," said Hill. "Georgia Tech plans to sue us for breach of contract unless we either pay them three thousand dollars or play the game."

George was devastated. For the past few days he had consoled himself with the idea that things would work out. That all would be forgiven, and that life would go on without a hitch.

"I'm not sure what this means for our school at this time," Hill told George. "We don't have the funds to spare. If we pay this, Cumberland University will likely go bankrupt. But I see no other choice."

George, sick to the pit of his stomach, was stunned and couldn't believe a wealthy school like Georgia Tech would not let them off the hook, after all, it was just a football game.

He tossed a series of questions to President Hill.

"What do you think is driving this? Who is making the decision for Tech? Is it Coach Heisman or the president? How much time do we have?"

It was that last question that would take precedence.

Who is calling the signals?

As President Hill began to address the dilemma, he began with George's initial inquiry.

"I have to believe Coach Heisman is behind it," Hill said. "You know better than anyone how angry he was last spring when you put together that baseball team that embarrassed him. He was livid, and if my memory serves me correctly, after that game he vowed he

Georgia Tech President
Kenneth Matheson

would get even. This, my young friend, is pure and unadulterated revenge."

But there may have been more to it than one man's wrath.

There were many characteristics shared by Georgia Tech President Kenneth Matheson and Coach John Heisman. Both men were stern, driven and determined and had built their reputations on the demand for self-discipline. They saw the world in black and white with no gray in between. Their answer to any question was either yes or no. They had a zero tolerance for human error.

The fifty-two-year-old Matheson had spent most of his professional career in education in college and prep-school military programs.

Born July 28, 1864, in Cheraw, South Carolina, Matheson graduated from The Citadel in 1885. His tenure as a student there very much shaped his adult life. He learned and practiced values associated with rigid discipline. He learned to polish brass, shine shoes, starch uniforms and make a serious commitment to academics.

He served as the commandant of cadets at Georgia Military College in Milledgeville, Georgia; at the University of Tennessee in Knoxville; and at the Missouri Military Academy in Mexico, Missouri. He earned a master's degree in English from Stanford University before accepting a job as a junior professor of English at Georgia Tech in 1897. Promoted to full professor the following year, he was appointed acting president of the school in 1905. In 1906 he was officially made president of Georgia Tech, a role he held until 1922.

Matheson's life was governed by principles associated with military discipline. His patience was limited when it came to students mixing a social life with academics. Study came first, second and third.

Heisman and Matheson were cut from the same cloth.

Heisman had a specific regimen when it came to matters of discipline, following rules, work ethic, and doing things the right way.

He was rigid but fair. He expected the best efforts from his players, and he believed the passion they held for their sport should be every bit as strong and fervent as his own.

Heisman came to Georgia Tech in 1904 at the age of thirty-five. His sights were set on a national championship and had not dimmed.

So, who was forcing the game?

Perhaps it was both.

No other option

President Hill and George began to evaluate their options. Hill took the matter to the members of the University's board of trust. The response he got was not one of understanding.

Board members, realizing the school was at risk of financial failure, wanted answers. They wanted to know why Tech had not been given adequate notice about the cancellation of the football schedule and they wanted to know who was to blame.

They ordered Hill to report three days later at special meeting at two o'clock Friday afternoon. So he had but three days to strategize and present all the options.

Confiding in George, President Hill told him about the meeting and stressed how serious this case was proving to be. It could be a matter of life or death for the lauded law school that had survived the Civil War half a century ago.

It was the great war between North and South that had planted Cumberland in the shadows of Harvard and Yale. While the Ivy League schools thrived after the conflict between the states, Cumberland barely limped along. When the war broke out Cumberland faculty members and students were divided in their allegiance.

Several professors left their teaching posts to assume leadership positions in the conflict. Most notable of these men was Gen. A.P. Stewart, who became one of the South's most respected tacticians.

Even now the division on campus had not been resolved, as many of the students had fathers, uncles and grandfathers who fought on one side or the other. And as for the local boys, they still harbored hard feelings over the thought of Union troops

Confederate Gen. Alexander P. Stewart

burning of the university's main building.

After the war Cumberland struggled to attract students. Students from the North had little desire to enroll in the law school because of fear of reprisal, while many students in the South had no money to pay their expenses.

The 1865 law class had only eleven students, one of them an ex-Confederate general and another a former Union colonel.

In 1866 the school adopted the image of the phoenix, the mythological Egyptian bird that arose from its own ashes along with the mantra "E Cineribus Resurgo" which translates "I rise from the ashes."

These were tough times indeed for Cumberland, and one more major setback could serve as the final blow.

Time for a decision

Three days passed, and the scheduled football game between Cumberland University and Georgia Tech was three weeks away.

Neither George nor President Hill had been idle. They scrambled for a solution that might satisfy Tech but so far had only come up with goose eggs.

Would Tech accept a second apology? Neither thought that ploy would succeed.

After all this was shaping up to be Heisman's year. Georgia Tech was contending for the national title. His team's schedule appeared to be a coach's dream with the pushovers first, followed by the tougher opponents.

Tech would open the season September 30 playing Mercer. Next was to come Cumberland, followed by Davidson, North Carolina, Washington and Lee, and Tulane. Tech would either make or break their case for the national championship when they closed the final three weeks against the likes of Alabama, Georgia and Auburn.

To snare the coveted position, Heisman and his charges would have to run the board winning every game, thrashing their foes soundly. Sportswriters during the era were more inclined to base their opinions about the strength of college teams on the number of points a team scored against an opponent. That meant that lopsided victories played a major role in determining the national champion. So coaches often mopped up against weaker schools, scoring anywhere from fifty to seventy points against the patsies.

Heisman faced another dilemma. Football teams in the South did not receive the same esteem as those in the Northeast. Sportswriters, mainly ensconced at large metropolitan dailies in the Northeast were prejudiced against the quality of the game in the South.

For Heisman to attract their attention and nominate his team for top honors, he was forced to show no mercy when it came to piling up the points. Cumberland, he figured, was a perfect candidate to play into his hands.

Hill, no slouch, contacted a tribe of legal scholars, all Cumberland graduates, hoping they might find a loophole in the contract that would allow an escape. These men scrutinized the document and came to one conclusion: play or pay.

The clock was ticking.

It was noon on Friday, and salvation appeared nowhere in sight.

A last-minute reprieve?

About an hour before the board meeting was to be called to order at two o'clock, George knocked on the president's door. Hill sat behind his large walnut desk with his hands folded. His countenance appeared to be that of a soldier about to surrender.

George asked for permission to enter.

Hill reluctantly invited him in. He could not imagine that the student could save the day and have a plan as to how they could come up with three thousand dollars.

"What is it?" Hill gruffly asked George. "I don't have a lot of time. I've got to come up with some answers rather quickly."

"I have an idea. I know it's asinine but this can work. And I'm sure I can put it together," George gushed.

Desperate for any way out, Hill urged George to spill it.

"I think we should play the game, he said with an angelic smile.

"How can that be?" the president asked, grasping for the straw before him.

"Let me address the board. Let me tell them how we can pull this off, said George.

Hill nodded affirmatively. He knew that ultimately the burden rested on his shoulders. He should have confirmed that all the schools on this fall's schedule had been notified of Cumberland's decision to eliminate football.

"OK, George, here's how it will go down. I'll go in first, open the meeting and begin our proceedings. Once we take roll and establish that a quorum is present, I'll briefly recant the issue, advise trustees that there might be a solution. At that point I will call you in, introduce you and explain your role," said the man on the hot seat.

Cumberland will play

"Members of the board of trust," Hill began, "we're here today considering this predicament due to my own negligence. Georgia Tech apparently will not retreat from its demand that we play a scheduled football game or pay their institution the sum of three thousand dollars.

"You will recall that last spring you voted to halt the school's football program in an effort to strengthen our beloved institution's financial profile. You entrusted me with the duties to carry out this decision so as to meet all legal commitments and obligations.

"I confess that I failed to meet your expectation and compromised your trust and confidence in me as president of this University. For my failures I am truly sorrowful and remorseful," Hill shared.

He then transformed the gloomy atmosphere of the affair by offering a glimmer of hope.

Introducing George to the group of wealthy businessmen, professors, and members of the bar and judiciary, Hill said, "I want to bring to your attention an outstanding young law student who is a gifted leader and who has been a valuable confidant to the service of my office since he first arrived on campus.

"I don't know how many of you have made the acquaintance of George Allen, but allow me to tell you that, although his grades may not substantiate it, he is one of the brightest students in his law class. He has been invaluable in serving us as a messenger to his fellow students, whether the news be good or bad.

"He performed yeoman's duty in explaining to his classmates justifying why we took actions, cost-saving measures, in order to preserve Cumberland's superior academic standing.

"You may recall that last spring he orchestrated in a matter of days a baseball game that involved our students and a large portion of the Lebanon community. That game was George's idea to show students that our decision to eliminate football was not a death blow to student life on campus. To George's credit and to the pleasure of those attending that game, our baseball team crushed Georgia Tech 22–0, a squad coached by Tech's football coach John Heisman.

"Our boys' win was Tech's worst defeat of the spring. Ironically, we're here today to deal with another game involving Georgia Tech, which, if not remedied, could spell doom for this school.

"Gentlemen, George believes he has a cure for our ailing situation. I have asked him to share his intentions."

The twenty-year-old law student from rural Mississippi took his position behind the speaker's podium. He gazed around the room taking a moment to mentally organize his thoughts. Clearing his throat, he had one simple statement to make.

"Sirs, on October 7th, the 1916 Cumberland University football team will play Georgia Tech."

"But how can this be," the board quizzed in unison, knowing the school had no uniforms or equipment, and, more to the point, no players.

"Trust me," George urged. "I will make it happen."

CHAPTER
FIVE

CHANGING THE GAME AND THE RULES

Things to be done

For the first time in his life, the unflappable George Allen found himself facing a marathon list of chores that caused even him to wonder what he had gotten himself into, all for the sake of a letter he forgot to write.

Consumed by his law school studies, the overwhelmed lad knew he had three weeks to organize a football team, scrape up uniforms and equipment, and plan transportation for an unlikely gridiron gang to Atlanta.

At the top of his list of things to do was how to communicate to Georgia Tech that the game would be played.

On Saturday morning, the day after the board meeting, George strolled over to the president's home. He discovered President Hill sipping a cup of coffee while meandering around the remains of his summer garden.

"So, exactly what is your plan, George?" Hill inquired.

"The plan is still in the making, sir," replied George, adding that he was not there to discuss how he would produce a team, much less have them prepared to play a powerhouse, but he was seeking wisdom from the president on the best way to notify Tech that Cumberland would be set for the kick-off on the first Saturday in October.

The two talked for a short while and decided to inform the Tech president and its football coach that the Bulldogs would make their word good.

"We don't want any errors on this. We need to be clear that Cumberland intends to fulfill its contractual obligation and will report to play Georgia Tech as agreed," Hill said.

Hill told George to concoct the message as succinctly as possible and to send it by Western Union as well as with a letter via the U.S. mail.

George did as he was instructed.

His letter to President Matheson and Coach Heisman simply stated, "Cumberland University, the South's finest educational institution, will field a football team on October 7, 1916, and be in Atlanta, Georgia, to play Georgia Tech, as provided by contract."

He closed the letter with four short words that froze a blank stare on Heisman's face for a full thirty seconds. The declaration? "We plan to win."

Skullduggery afoot?

Preposterous might describe the first notion that shot through the stunned coach's brain.

How could a tiny school like Cumberland dream of holding its own on the field with a formidable foe like mighty Tech?

Heisman scratched his chin and shook his head. "They must be crazy," he thought.

But then again, somehow last spring Heisman recalled, Cumberland, loaded with a bench full of semi-pros, knocked the socks off his ranked baseball squad.

Heisman wondered if this guy George Allen could pull such a miracle a second time.

Heisman also thought back to his disappointment in 1903 when his Clemson team fought Cumberland to an 11–11 tie in the title game for the Southern Intercollegiate Athletic Association football championship. That same year his Clemson Tigers shocked Georgia Tech 73–0, and by next fall he was Tech's head coach.

His first season at Georgia Tech ended November 24, 1904, on a home field in Atlanta with an 18–0 win over Cumberland. Heisman's team repeated that feat the next year by the same score.

Heisman's history

Despite battling him twice on the gridiron and once on the diamond, Cumberland University knew little about John Heisman.

It was true that he was a single-minded, hard-driving football and baseball coach who was consumed with winning. But there was far more to the intelligent and imaginative coach.

John William Heisman was born in Cleveland, Ohio, on October 23, 1869 (two weeks before the first football game was played between Princeton and Rutgers), and died in New York City at age 66 years on October 3, 1936, after a short bout with pneumonia.

The headline of *The New York Times* obituary said in two stacked lines 'John W. Heisman, Noted Coach Dies,' and reported only that he died at home and that his death came "after a brief illness." On October 6 his body was placed on a train and taken to Rhineland, Wisconsin, where he was laid to rest in his wife's hometown.

At the time of his death he held the post of physical director at New York's Downtown Athletic Club. Since 1935 that organization has presented the most prestigious award in college football,

The Heisman Trophy

the Heisman Trophy, to the college player "whose performance best exhibits the pursuit of excellence with integrity."

Though outsized by those playing against him, Heisman, at 5'8" and 158 pounds, got his first taste of college football at age 17 playing a combination of line positions including guard, tackle, center and sometimes end for Brown University in 1887. After two years at Brown, he transferred to the University of Pennsylvania in the fall of 1889, where he played varsity football for three years and earned a degree in law in 1892.

He landed his first head coaching job as the football coach at Oberlin College, a private liberal arts college in Oberlin, Ohio, at age 23 and held that position from 1892 to 1894.

Heisman's resume also included coaching stints at Buchtel, today the University of Akron (1893–1894); Auburn (1895–1899); Clemson (1900–1903); Georgia Tech (1904–1919); the University of Pennsylvania (1920–1922); Washington and Jefferson College (1923); and Rice (1924–1927).

He compiled a remarkable record by today's standards of 186 wins, 70 losses, and 18 ties. Only at Rice was he unable to accrue a winning record. He won a national championship at Georgia Tech in 1917 after posting a perfect 9–0 season.

The cagey coach proved to have one of the most innovative minds in the game, and sportswriters looked upon him as a scientist because of the plays and stunts he brought to the sport.

He introduced a scheme where two pulling guards led blockers on an end run; created what is known as the "Heisman Shift," a precursor to the "T" formation; originated the center snap; and was first to instruct his quarterbacks to shout "hike!" or "hep1" to signal the center to snap the ball and begin the play.

Heisman came up with the hidden ball trick, quickly banned, where a running back would tuck the pigskin beneath under his jersey; double passes or laterals in the backfield; reverse pitches on running plays; and signaling plays to the team on the field from the sideline.

His inspirations often led to the need for rule changes and new rules.

He once had the image of a football painted on the front of his team's jerseys, a ploy to confuse the defense as to which running back was being handed the ball in the offensive backfield.

Violence in the game

Football had become so violent in the early 1900s that many called for the sport to be abolished. Even President Theodore Roosevelt showed concern over the injuries and asked that those involved in the sport find ways to reduce the physical dangers. Several players had been killed in 1905 on the playing field, three in one day, and that led to even stronger pleas that something be done to stop the violence.

Heisman took the lead along with Yale athletic director Walter Camp, whose rules of the game were endorsed and followed nationally. He asked Camp to consider legalizing the forward pass, believing that would reduce much of the roughness on the line of scrimmage, loosen up the game overall and make it safer for players.

The forward pass, Heisman's brainchild, was legalized in 1906.

In his efforts to revamp the sport and make it less dangerous, Heisman also is recognized as being responsible for having games divided into quarters. Originally, the game had but a half-time division.

For his wizardry, on and off the field, he was inducted into the College Football Hall of Fame in 1954.

On the side Heisman proved a credible college baseball coach, amassing a record of 219–119–7 at three schools: Buchtel, Clemson and Georgia Tech.

THE FORWARD PASS

It's believed that John Heisman observed the forward pass demonstrated for the first time while he was scouting a game between the universities of Georgia and North Carolina in 1895.

When a punter in the game fumbled the snap from center, he managed to grasp the pigskin just enough to heave it forward across the line of scrimmage to a teammate who caught the ball and sped for a touchdown.

Despite the desperation of the wobbly fling, Heisman recognized this was a play that could dramatically change the game.

Heisman may not have invented the forward pass, but he was its chief cheerleader and saw that it became a legal offensive option. He also believed that it would prevent costly injuries on the line of scrimmage.

Between 1904 and 1905 forty-four players were reported killed while playing football, and hundreds of others suffered serious injuries. The viciousness of the sport had gotten out of hand. Heisman wrote that the bruising, running game was "killing the game as well as the players."

Arguing for the rule change, he said the forward pass "would scatter the mob," meaning that the monstrous turmoil surrounding running plays could be greatly relieved.

Continued

He lobbied Walter Camp at Yale, the man regarded as the keeper of the rules for college football during that era, to make the forward pass legal. Camp did not react initially, thus Heisman promoted his campaign nationwide, stirring support from coaches and sportswriters.

Camp acquiesced in 1906. The forward pass became legal, and the game of football was changed forever in a good way.

The thespian

There were occasions when Heisman taught the game of football to his players as if he was producing a Broadway play.

The coach was passionate over the works of Shakespeare and often spent summers performing in plays. He was enthralled with acting and singing.

He had a habit of using polysyllabic language when speaking about or coaching football, a trait he had mastered from his love of Shakespeare and his Ivy League education in law at the University of Pennsylvania.

Practicing his Shakespearean speech he would regularly welcome a new flock of athletes by holding a football in front of his audience and asking, "Do you know what this is?""

Then, providing an answer to his own question he would explain, "It is a prolate spheroid in which the outer leather casing is drawn tightly over a somewhat smaller rubber tubing."

Then he would pause, gaze eye to eye with the players before him and offer, "Better to have died as a small boy than to fumble this football."

Following his theatrical bent in 1897, Heisman produced, directed and was an actor in a play to benefit the Auburn athletic department which was floundering in debt because of its football program.

The coach, who had been an actor in New York before coming to Auburn, succeeded in raising nearly $700, which served to persuade school administrators to field a football team the next year.

Not much time

George Allen stretched out on the couch in the Kappa Sig frat house with a load on his mind.

He had pledged himself as the principle collateral on a performance contract that, if not fulfilled, could bring down his alma mater.

"What in the hell am I going to do?" George muttered to himself.

It was late on a Friday afternoon and the fraternity house was already beginning to buzz. Frat brothers, their sweethearts, and friends were scattered inside the house, out on the porch, and sitting beneath huge shade trees on this humid, warm September day.

Several of his comrades, enjoying a cold brew disguised in an outdated dark canning jar, noticed George was not wearing the easy countenance or beaming smile that typically dominated his face.

Gingerly, some of his house brothers approached him, thinking maybe he was having problems with his studies or that he had gotten into a confrontation with a professor.

"Hey, George. How's it going?" asked his pal Gentry, a friend of George whose name he subconsciously filed at the top of the list of students he planned to coerce into playing in the game against Tech.

Calculating his response, as he didn't want to tip his hand at this early stage, George said simply, "We need to talk later."

While he went upstairs to change clothes, the conversation among the young folks below turned to speculation on their friend's hushed behavior.

HEISMAN QUOTES

"To break training without permission is an act of treason."

"Don't cuss. Don't argue with the officials. And don't lose the game."

"Gentlemen, it is better to have died a small boy than to fumble this football."

"When you find your opponent's weak spot, hammer it."

"When in doubt, punt!"

A few minutes later George came down, grabbed a bottle of beer from the ice box and rejoined the crowd. After downing the drink he asked the congenial congregation to step outside. Holding forth on the front porch, he addressed the group of about 50 mostly male students.

"This has been an interesting day," he began, choosing his words carefully. "I am facing a challenge of gigantic proportion. By Monday it's going to involve all of us in one degree or another. I need some time to meditate on the matter and to devise a plan, but when I reach a resolution, I am going to need the support of each one of you as well as others. Please be on alert.

"I can say that in the years ahead you will have the exquisite honor of telling your children and grandchildren that when you were a student at Cumberland University you raised your hand and volunteered for a noble deed. You saved the school you loved."

Then George retreated inside for a few minutes and moments later hopped into his Chevy and drove away. He needed a solitary place to conspire. He had to find a way to get Cumberland back on the football field, if only for one last game.

CHAPTER
SIX

GEORGE AND JACK TIE ONE ON

A trip to Nashville

George drove his automobile around Lebanon for a couple of hours. As sundown approached, he knew the last place he needed to be was with his cohorts at the Kappa Sig house.

He struggled to come up with a site that would offer a retreat where he could concentrate.

On a whim he turned west on to the Nashville Highway. Soon he passed the turn off to Horn Springs. That was another spot he needed to avoid. He motored on, past the sleepy village of Mt. Juliet, past Hermitage and Donelson and nearly two hours later, he cruised into the capitol city of Nashville.

Heading downtown, he made a few turns and found himself on Sixth Avenue. Looking to his left, he spied the logical solution to his dilemma: the Hermitage Hotel.

Opened in 1910, the hotel would make a haven and head-quarters for George to layout his master plan.

Hermitage Hotel

HERMITAGE HOTEL

Requiring two full years for construction, the hotel, listed in the National Register of Historical Places, represents a Beaux-Arts style of architecture. Situated only two blocks from the Tennessee Capitol, the Hermitage Hotel has been the hotel of choice for a number of U.S. presidents when visiting Nashville including Howard Taft, Woodrow Wilson, John Kennedy, Lyndon Johnson, and Richard Nixon. The hotel took its name from the plantation home of President Andrew Jackson and has been the meeting place for legislators, decision makers, and the state's powerful elite since its early days.

The rack rate for a one-night stay was three dollars. He booked himself in at the front desk for two nights.

Beer was out of the question, but there was no reason to keep George from ordering a pint of Jack Daniels from one of the hotel's bell hops, gents who doubled as metropolitan bootleggers.

He inquired about the price of a pint of Jack's "Old No. 7."

Advised he could get his order delivered to the room for two bucks, a steep tab when you considered a gallon of Jack Daniels only cost $3.50 legally. But nonetheless George placed an order.

Ninety minutes later he heard a knock on his hotel room door. Outside a young African-American cradled a brown paper sack crunched around his libation of choice.

George paid the man and turned his attention to serious drinking and thinking.

One sip at a time

George chatted aloud with his mute friend Jack, who slouched in the six-ounce glass by the student manager's side.

After taking his first swallow, the master planner reached into the center desk drawer of the Louis IVX-styled library table, a standard guest room fixture at the Hermitage, and pulled out four sheets of the hotel's smartly-embossed stationery.

He began scribbling, then doodling before he wrote down five words in capital letters: TEAM, EQUIPMENT, TRANSPORTATION, EXPENSES, LOGISTICS.

These terms would dictate the outline of his master plan and keep his mind on track while he dallied with his old friend Jack into the early hours of Saturday morning. He would take a sip, write a few words and then repeat the process.

After racking his brain for most of the night and consuming his pint of whiskey, George wasn't any closer to a solution than when he was driving around the Lebanon square the evening before.

By now the first rays of sunshine were sneaking through the window blinds.

George thought it best to lay down his pen, step outside for some fresh air, have a hearty breakfast, embellished with a pot of coffee to get the adrenalin going.

After dining he retreated to his room and did not invite pal Jack to what he conceived would be a well disciplined planning session.

First up, he tackled the major problem of how Cumberland could construct a football team out of thin air.

He briefly wondered if he might repeat the stunt he pulled last spring and nab a band of ringers in Nashville. There could be some strapping former high school athletes, who might sign on for an intriguing and competitive adventure in Atlanta and the opportunity to step into their cleats for one more game.

And George also could put some feelers out to Vanderbilt University to see if any of its players had an itching to tackle some brainy boys at Tech.

He was confident he could make an attractive pitch if he could locate the prospects.

Staying close to home

As the morning slipped into early afternoon, George agonized over his dilemma. Eventually he came to the conclusion that the bulk of the players should be Cumberland men.

He could start with Gentry and a couple of other fraternity brothers whom he could trust to not let the secret slip until he'd finished his master plan.

He then sat down to map out the details.

By Sunday morning he had several pages filled with notes. George had created an organizational chart and spent the rest of the day filling in the blanks, including the names of potential players.

He also had a list of tasks. He would assign some of his non-athletic buddies to handle many of these jobs.

As for football equipment, he figured he could scrape up the jerseys from last year's team and filch some pads and helmets from Castle Heights Military Academy, the military prep school a half mile away from Cumberland. He would gather a half-dozen footballs from frat houses and students.

To get his squad to Atlanta the only practical means of transport would be passenger train. There were three rail routes between Nashville and Atlanta frequently traveled. One took passengers east to Knoxville and from Knoxville south to Atlanta. The second route went from Nashville to Birmingham and from Birmingham east to Atlanta. And the third was directed from Nashville to Chattanooga and then one-hundred miles south to Atlanta.

The smart thing to do, George thought, would be to board the train in Lebanon, loading the equipment in the same car with the players and accompanying students. That guaranteed that all would arrive together.

He would decide on which route once he got the price of the tickets and schedule. There also would be the expense of staying two nights in an Atlanta hotel and meals.

With his ragamuffin scheme seemingly coming together, the bushed schemer hit the hay late Saturday night.

Back to school

George checked out of the Hermitage Hotel shortly before noon Sunday and cruised back to Lebanon, pulling up to the frat house around two o'clock.

There he was greeted by Gentry and his band of brothers. They had been fretting about his mental state ever since he disappeared on Friday.

They quickly recognized that George was back to his same old self as he was laughing and asking about the weekend's social affairs.

After things calmed down, George tapped Gentry on the shoulder and pulled him aside for a private chat.

He revealed the mystery to Gentry, going through the whole story beginning with him being the one who screwed things up by forgetting to tell Georgia Tech that Cumberland would not be fielding a team.

George explained how he and the president had convinced the board of trust a few days earlier that they would get a team together and make good on the contract with Tech. He told Gentry that they gave their word that the Cumberland Bulldogs would be on Georgia Tech's field in Atlanta in three weeks, would fulfill their obligation to Tech, and that their efforts would serve to remove the Lebanon school from the cloud of financial disruption being threatened.

GENTRY DUGAT: *The Cumberland alum is remembered as a colorful Texas historian, orator, and journalist. Born on a ranch outside of Beeville, Texas, Dugat earned a degree in law from Cumberland University, worked on seven Texas newspapers, edited the Cotton Ginners Journal, and wrote a biography of post Civil War editor and orator Henry W. Grady. In 1958 the World War I veteran organized the Bee County, Texas Historical Commission.*

He only asked that Gentry keep it a secret until Monday afternoon when he planned to call together the student body for a rally on the front lawn of Memorial Hall.

With Gentry's help, George began spreading word about the rendezvous. Handbills written in bright red on notebook paper were posted around the campus. Messengers were sent to every dorm room to invite resident students.

By noon Monday word had seeped throughout Lebanon that George Allen would be making a big announcement at three o'clock on the Cumberland campus.

Everyone in town recognized George's name, as he was the guy who had promoted the big baseball game the spring before against Georgia Tech when the Bulldogs topped Heisman's ranked team 22–0.

What on God's green earth could George be up to this time?

CHAPTER
SEVEN

MAKING IT HAPPEN

A crowd gathers

An hour before George was to make his announcement, the front lawn of the Cumberland University campus had already taken the appearance of an old-time religious tent meeting. While most were standing, some women had spread blankets beneath shade trees, and some had brought heavy, wooden folding chairs. The hundred or so congregated were college students for the most part with a dozen or more being townsfolk.

One hour later, the gathering had swollen considerably, closing in on a thousand curious souls.

By this time, the attendees included a few members of the board of trust, faculty members, law school professors and a good showing from citizens of Lebanon.

Watching from the president's window in Memorial Hall, the same window from which Gen. Patton would years later look over troops of the Second Army, George tried to focus on his speech but the blossoming crowd distracted him.

Cumberland Memorial Hall

He forced himself to turn away and went over his notes one final time.

Despite graduating next to last in a class of 178 law students, George was quick witted and had a special gift for gab when it came to holding the attention of an audience of 200 or for that matter a frat house gathering of a couple of dozen.

But this time the occasion was different. It wasn't a joke he was to tell or some amusing anecdote.

This time he would be espousing a message about the prospects and the process to ensure Cumberland's survival.

Plan of action

Precisely at three, George nervously stepped outside and took his stance on the front steps. He leaned forward as he began his oration, his voice cracking as he confessed that a few months back he had made a grave error, a mistake that may have placed "this great University" in a state of financial jeopardy.

Continuing to take the blame, he explained that it had been his responsibility as team manager to notify the schools on Cumberland's football schedule that the University had decided to disband its football program and would not be fielding a team in the fall of 1916. He spoke plainly and honestly as he told the listeners that he had accidentally failed to provide this notice to Georgia Tech.

His demeanor became graver as he told the crowd about the harsh financial consequences due to his blunder and the insistence on the part of Tech that the football game be played or else.

Finally, he reminded the now silent and stunned gathering that the baseball game played last spring against Tech had whipped up a tempest as the Bulldogs had drubbed Coach Heisman's Tech team so soundly.

"Coach Heisman has nurtured one of the toughest football teams in the nation," said George. "He plans to settle for nothing less than the national championship, and it messes up his schedule and likely weakens his opportunity should we forfeit our game. He has demanded that Cumberland play Tech on Grant Field in Atlanta in less than three weeks or he will take his pound of flesh via three thousand greenback dollars.

"If we forfeit, the odds increase that our beloved alma mater will have to shutter her doors. I cannot bear to imagine that such a blow come upon this school, an educational giant that has overcome previous hardships, including a torching that disintegrated an earlier headquarters, yet Cumberland survived to rise again from ashes. I feel quite sure that you all feel the same as I.

"Therefore, I pronounce to you today that come hail or high water, Cumberland will produce a football team and play Tech in Atlanta on October 7."

Scrambling to get organized

Following the speech, students rushed to the front of the majestic Memorial Hall and volunteered to help in whatever way they could to assist the cause.

George's priority was to draft sixteen to twenty athletes. He realized some of them may never have played organized football before, and there were strong possibilities that a match like this against Heisman's stable of athletes could result in broken noses, broken arms, broke ribs and broken skulls.

Tech was a big boy team, composed of men, not fraternity boys. Poised to become national champions, they were superbly trained and conditioned.

George first cast his line for players inside his pond of fraternity brothers. He reasoned that if he could snare four or five Kappa Sigma volunteers, he could hit on the other frat houses and coerce each of them to supply a couple of workhorses.

Part of his pitch was the notion that the journey to Atlanta would prove an unforgettable adventure, a historical event. Moving in to close the sale, he leaned on their emotions. He lectured that the game to be played was not so much about whom would win or if Tech and Heisman would capture their national championship, but that it would be a signature event that would determine the salvation of Cumberland University.

"Fifty years from now, when you are old and your grandsons surround you, you can take great pride in telling them that you were one of a small band of brothers who fought a gallant and glorious battle against a giant and did so with honor. This gentlemen is the chance of a lifetime."

Two volunteers stepped forward immediately from the Kappa Sig family. Gentry Dugat and Morris Gouger, who played high school football in their home state of Texas, were ready, willing and able.

Next Leon McDonald and George Murphy said they'd make the trip. Then Eddie Edwards and Charlie Warwick also agreed to play.

George was a bit surprised that his first try at raising a team has claimed a half dozen willing want-to-be athletes. He was almost halfway home with his roster.

Raising the money

Once George began to tabulate the expenses of getting his small army to Atlanta, he totaled the costs to be approximately five hundred dollars, not exactly chicken feed.

When Gentry asked him how he planned to get his hands on that much dough, George quipped, "I'm fixin' to raise more money then I'll probably ever see in my lifetime."

He set his first bull's-eye on the men of the Cumberland Board of Trust. Most were wealthy local businessmen and lawyers, while a few were professors. From the fifteen, he believed he could secure the first hundred.

A couple of the trustees were reputed to be loaded. A.W. Hooker operated a successful lumberyard and provided most of the building materials for residential and business construction in

Lebanon. Walter J. Baird also was a prosperous businessman and property owner.

George's fundraising scheme called for ten coeds to go door-to-door to businesses and residences across the community asking for anything from a quarter to two dollars. He figured that would bring in two hundred.

Another fifty bucks could be raised from a sorority cake and cookie sale on the Saturday the week before the game.

Finally, for those looking for a somewhat more rousing way to give, George had begged for the assistance of the owner of the Devil's Elbow on the square for a raucous Friday night keg party, an event that would feature all the beer a man could drink, complimented by pickled eggs, for two dollars.

George estimated that a week before the game, he should have harvested more than four hundred dollars, an amount meeting the bare minimum to make the trip. With any luck at all, he would raise the entire five hundred and even have enough cash to treat the team to a steak dinner in Atlanta after the game.

Getting closer to game day

It had been ten days since George announced to the student body that the football game with Georgia Tech was going to take place.

His ragtag army of athletes had been assembled, although it could still use a few more bodies. Most of the money had been raised, uniforms had been secured, and this week George would purchase train tickets, make hotel reservations, and tidy up unfinished business so he could dedicate more time to focusing on Cumberland's game strategy.

Technically, George did not serve as coach, as that person had to be a member of the University faculty, thus Ernest (Butch) McQueen filled those shoes on paper, while George truly took charge.

The game strategy would not be so much about scoring points or even winning, but instead the big question was how could Cumberland's players get through four quarters of football against a Tech behemoth and walk away with heads held high and health intact?

CHAPTER
EIGHT

DOWN IN
ATLANTA

Looking like a championship year

The outlook for Coach John Heisman in his twelfth year at Georgia Tech was splendid.

Although Tech's 1916 season would not kick off until September 30, he was confident he had the horses to win a national championship.

In the previous season Tech had posted a record of seven victories, no losses and a scoreless tie against the University of Georgia near the end of the schedule. Until that point Tech considered itself a contender as the top team in the country despite the prejudices of the national press.

However, Cornell, coached by Albert Sharpe, with a perfect 9–0 record, shared national championship honors that year with Glen Scobey "Pop" Warner's Pittsburgh Panthers, which produced an 8–0 season.

Tech's 1915 team caught glances from the national press as it defeated Mercer, Davidson, Transylvania, LSU, North Carolina, Alabama and Auburn. But sportswriters shared the opinion that the strength of collegiate football lay in the North and Northeast.

Fred Russell, sports editor of the Nashville Banner, and Grantland Rice share a conversation in 1951

Because Heisman's Georgia Tech team had gained a wink or so of national recognition for its campaign in 1915, the stage was set many in Atlanta believed for a national champion to be named from the South in 1916.

Coach Heisman and his budding football dynasty at Tech were beginning to make themselves known on the national stage and gaining the attention from a corps of well-respected sportswriters across America. Among those closely following Heisman was Grantland Rice, the famed sportswriter, who at this time anchored the "sporting news" section of the *New York Tribune*.

Rice, who had written for *The Atlanta Journal* during Heisman's early days at Tech, had observed the coach perform both on and off the field. Years later, the two developed a close friendship and co-authored the book, "Understand Football," in 1932.

Southern sportswriters had been covering the gridiron exploits by Heisman for some time, so with Rice in the Big Apple

HEISMAN'S BOOK

Following his tenure at Tech John Heisman wrote and published "Principles of Football,' a best-seller among football coaches and players and still a popular read for many associated with the game.

Amazon, a vender of the book, offers "The bedrock simplicity of legendary coach John Heisman's 'Principles of Football' will knock the wind out of you like a four-man tackle deep behind the line of scrimmage. Originally published in the 1920s, this classic is perfect for every young player and coach, as well as all lovers of the game. The book includes more than 40 of Heisman's plays; insight to Heisman's innovative, no-loss attitude; time-tested and timeless tips on merging game strategy with gentlemanly sportsmanship to teach how to master the 'mental game;' and. a complete listing of Heisman Trophy recipients, plus John Heisman's 175 basic football axioms."

95

the eastern side of the nation was gaining a bit of knowledge about the hard-nosed wizard in Atlanta.

Disappointed by the 1915 campaign, Heisman would not stand for anything less than stellar play this year and was determined that his squad play every game as if it were for a national title.

He admonished his players to look upon each opponent as a foe that could take them down and out of contention for the prized goal if they did not strive for perfection. He warned them against making mental mistakes, that running backs and receivers hold tightly to the ball, and that they play sound and aggressive defense.

The Cumberland game would be Tech's second of the season, and like every game on the schedule it was a must win if they were to claim the national title.

There should be no way in kingdom come for Cumberland to threaten much less beat Tech this year. But when Coach Heisman reflected on that disappointing baseball game last spring in Lebanon, even he had to pause and wonder what if.

Confident that the baseball debacle occurred due to Cumberland using a batch of ringers, he was not about to let anything like that happen again when Tech played the Tennessee team on their home field.

Keeping his team focused, Coach Heisman conducted practice sessions and planned strategy as if Tech was about to face an equal. He would take nothing for granted when it came to the small school, which he intended to give a serious butt whipping.

Back in Lebanon

Things were falling into place for George Allen and his Bulldogs.

The team and the travel party, which would number nearly a hundred, planned to board the train early next Friday. The

THE GEORGIAN TERRACE

Much like the Hermitage Hotel in Nashville, The Georgian Terrace, located at 659 Peachtree Street NE, is an architectural masterpiece and still in business.

The ten-story structure of Moorish Revival, Beaux-Arts style was designed by architect William Lee Stoddart and built for a sum of $500,000. The hotel has been featured prominently as host site for a number of historic events. Among celebrity guests have been film stars, politicians, military leaders, and authors. Those who overnighted at the hotel include Clark Gable, Vivien Leigh, Tallulah Bankhead, Laurence Olivier, Claudette Colbert, Olivia de Havilland, Calvin Coolidge, John J. Pershing, Walt Disney, and F. Scott Fitzgerald. It also was where, in the 1920s, a young Arthur Murray, a student at Georgia Tech, began giving dance lessons.

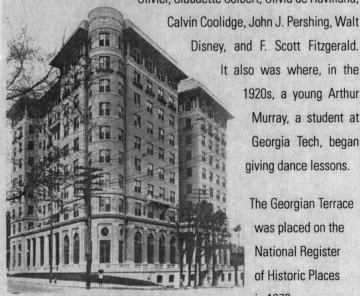

Atlanta Georgian Terrace Hotel

The Georgian Terrace was placed on the National Register of Historic Places in 1978.

seven-hour rail journey to Atlanta was being touted by George as one great celebration.

But secretly he was concerned that he may have oversold the deal. Wondering to himself he asked, "Surely, these folks realize that our team doesn't have a prayer."

On the Cumberland campus spirits raged with a jubilant atmosphere reminiscent of years past when Cumberland was a contender as one of the top teams in the country.

Sheets painted with such messages as "Wreck Tech," "Outsmart the Engineers," and "Bring Down the Gavel on Georgia Tech" hung from the dormitory windows. Posters covered bulletin boards in the hallways and classrooms.

The mayor of Lebanon organized a Main Street parade in the team's honor. Community churches joined hands with plans for a picnic lunch, a feast of barbecue, fried chicken, baked beans, potato salad, and homemade cakes and pies.

The fanfare leading up to the team's departure was more than George could have ever dreamed.

A final accounting showed that sufficient funds had been raised to finance the trip. George had his team in place, although he could use several more healthy bodies. Tickets had been purchased for fourteen players, one water boy, George and Coach McQueen. However, there were only a dozen players on the roster, George was praying fervently that he could roust three or four real players after the train stopped for a layover in Nashville.

Among others accompanying the team would be students, a few faculty members and administrators, and some of the wealthier town citizens, all on their own dime with respect to expenses.

The agenda called for the Cumberland squad to spend two nights in Atlanta at The Georgian Terrace, a superlative hotel that opened its doors in 1911. George, a young man of good taste, believed that if these students, football players for a day, were willing to risk their limbs for their school, they should be afforded billets in one of the grandest and newest hotels in the South.

The team and its entourage would arrive in Atlanta late on Friday afternoon and be escorted to the hotel by the Georgia Tech welcoming committee.

But for now George needed to huddle with his team, go over a few basic plays and prepare them mentally for four quarters of a football game that had all the potential to be a disaster.

Team meeting

George called his team together, a band of misfits that numbered fourteen, on Monday afternoon, five days away from game day.

They were legitimate Cumberland students, most of them studying law, a few liberal arts majors and several who had not yet decided their future livelihood nor selected a major.

George acknowledged that the players were students first, fraternity brothers second, party-goers third, and last and least, football players.

First, he passed out pads, pants, jerseys, helmets and cleats. After each student athlete suited up and settled, he had them sit down and went over the weekend schedule, from Friday morning until they returned on Sunday. He certainly didn't need any absentees.

Then he took questions from his young charges, who were not so much fearful as to what the Georgia Tech players could do to them in the trenches but were excited about their adventure to a major city in the South.

They wondered if they could bring their girlfriends, what foods they would be served, what they should wear, and how much money they needed to bring.

Those questions were easy for the overseer, but the last one was a challenge.

"George, I know we're doing something good here. I understand that and I'm glad to be a part of it," began a fraternity brother, who had kept his helmet on his head as if a gladiator prepared for battle.

"But what happens if one of us gets seriously hurt? Will we go to the hospital in Atlanta or will you tote us back to the train and take us to a doctor in Nashville? Will Cumberland pay our medical bill?"

"Men, I understand where your sentiments lay. I appreciate what you're doing for this school as I'm sure your fellow classmates, the professors and administration here, and the town of Lebanon do," said George.

"I think everything will work out fine. I think we'll go to Atlanta and play a crazy football game on Saturday. Spend the night in a magnificent hotel and come home on Sunday.

"We're probably not going to beat Georgia Tech. And it's my responsibility to make sure we get there and get back all in one piece. I can tell you right now, right here, that I will do my damn level best to make sure that you get the credit for your selfless commitment and that no one gets physically injured in the process."

The fourteen nodded affirmatively and went to the Cumberland football field for their first workout as a unit.

Second team meeting

George and the team met again on Tuesday afternoon to discuss strategy. He also preached to them to not get caught up in the hype.

"Look," he lectured, "we're simply going to Atlanta to have some fun, but don't do anything stupid. The only requirement before us is to show up and play a football game.

"We're doing this because of a contract. We don't have to win. We don't even have to score. We just want to fulfill our obligation and get off the field without injury."

George had designated Morris Gouger and Leon McDonald as quarterbacks as both had played the position in high school. They knew the essentials of the game and could fill in the blanks for some of the rookies, who were picking it up as they went along.

Third team meeting

At the third and final meeting George explained, "Guys this is it: our final practice before we reconvene Friday morning to board the train. Let's concentrate on our plays and what responsibilities each of you have at your respective positions."

Morris Gouger directed four basic running plays and also threw several short passes to both ends.

One play George had drawn up required Gouger to lateral the football to McDonald, and then McDonald would throw a long pass down field to the end. The play had been tagged "the Cumberland shuffle." The student manager thought if they could complete several passes, it could cut down on potential injuries.

Some of the plays conceived by George were given vegetable names like "green lettuce sweep" or "broccoli bash" to help players remember their individual assignments and to be able to recall which side of the line the play would be directed and who would be responsible for carrying the ball.

The team completed their final workout in two hours, retired to the dressing room and took off their equipment. The next time they dressed out, they would be facing Heisman and his horde of giants.

One last party

A final party was planned, a going-away celebration to be held at Horn Springs Thursday night. There'd be girls, dancing, alcoholic beverages and plenty of opportunities for members of the team to be led astray.

George couldn't afford to lose one player, but he didn't really have the wherewithal to keep his tribe in check. They were volunteers. George had absolutely nothing to hold them to their commitment, no leverage whatsoever. If they chose to not show up on Friday morning, there was really nothing he could do.

He awoke early Thursday morning and sat down at the frat house kitchen table for a big cup of hot coffee and to gather his thoughts for the day.

At eight a.m. he left for his first class. After finishing his last class at two o'clock he returned to the Kappa Sigma fraternity house.

Catching up with Gentry, he invited him to join him in the boiler room and coal storage area beneath Memorial Hall where the team equipment was stored.

Together they counted and recounted helmets, pants, jerseys, and pads to insure all were in place. Then, taking fourteen burlap potato sacks contributed by Eskew's Grocery, a local, family-owned store located only a few blocks off campus, they packed each sack with a complete ensemble, labeling each with the appropriate player's name.

An hour past sundown a number of students had already made their way to Horn Springs. A bonfire lay in wait for the heroes of the hour to arrive.

A small dance band with a decent vocalist played the popular tunes with a good blend of jazz singer Al Jolson's hits. Most of the evening the music proved festive, but as the night wore on, the songs took a turn toward the melancholy with some of the tunes proving patriotic in nature reflecting love of country. They easily could have been translated into love of Cumberland.

One such current popular hit was "The Star Spangled Banner." Written by Francis Scott Key one-hundred-and-two years earlier in 1814, the song, which would become the National Anthem in 1931, was being played by bands everywhere.

As the party roared on, more and more students arrived. The drum roll moment came when the fourteen football heroes exited their vehicles and began winding their way in single file through the crowd.

Shrieks, yells and cheers filled the air as the maddening celebration unfolded. The athletes ambled to the bonfire, where they were encircled by several hundred party-goers, and hurrahs were

TOP MUSIC SELECTIONS OF THE DAY

Billboard's top music selections in 1916 included "America," by the Columbia Mixed Quartet; "The Star Spangled Banner," by Prince's Orchestra; "The Battle Hymn of the Republic," by the Columbia Mixed Quartet; "Yaaka Hula Hickey Dula," by Al Jolson, "Good-bye, Good Luck, God Bless You," by Henry Burr; "The Sunshine of Your Smile," by John McCormack; "My Old Kentucky Home," by Adam Gluck; "O Sole Mio," by Enrico Caruso; "I Sent My Wife to the Thousand Isles," by Al Jolson; and in December the most popular tune was "Hark! the Herald Angels Sing," by The Columbia Mixed Quartet.

shouted by all as the fire was lit and the flames quickly brightened the dark steel blue night sky.

The party ran full tilt.

At two a.m. George thought it best to wind it down. He suggested to the bandleader that he play a couple of tunes that would signal to attendees that the party was on its last leg.

But first he wanted to make a few comments.

The band stopped, and for a brief moment the crowd hushed itself long enough for George to stumble through a few unrehearsed remarks. Taking a post immediately at the front of the raised gazebo/bandstand, George began, "We're here tonight celebrating, if you want to call it that, a selfless commitment that has been made by a few to benefit the many.

"These men didn't have to volunteer for this duty. But they did. They are laying on their shoulders the long and glorious history of our beloved university.

"I know you all join with me in saying thank you to each of these men.

"As we conclude this festive event, I'm asking that the band play two songs. Both say much about our country, and truly, I think about our school, about ourselves and about the privileges we have to be free and to be a part of something so great as a simple football game to be played for the salvation of our University."

George turned to the bandleader and requested "America," followed by "The Star Spangled Banner."

Day of departure

Friday morning made a grand entrance a mere few hours after the strains of "The Star Spangled Banner" had wound down. George did not have the luxury of getting a full eight hours of sleep.

He had his coffee and began knocking off a few last-minute details.

In the meantime, townspeople had been gathering at the train depot, a small wooden frame building a block off the Lebanon square and three or four blocks away from the campus. Merchants carried signs of support for the team. A group of students held a twenty-foot-long banner that read "Beat the Heck out of Georgia Tech."

The mammoth crowd numbered well over a thousand as they stood on their toes to watch the players board the train.

George stood next to the passenger car, checking his list one final time. He and Gentry had already made sure the fourteen potato sacks containing the players' equipment had been loaded.

He ticked off the last line on his lengthy check list and the final passenger boarded the train. The crowd cheered loudly as the train whistle gave a couple of blows, and slowly the Southern Railway iron horse chugged down the track.

DECISION NEAR IN 1915

Cumberland was nearing the decision of giving up football in 1915 but still hadn't quite pulled the trigger when it played Tennessee.

In the meantime a decision was made to play a limited four game schedule in 1915. If Cumberland hadn't made a decision to give up football by the beginning of the 1915 season, the question was surely decided by the season's end at least if winning or even being minimally competitive was a requirement. Cumberland lost all four games. Wofford beat the Bulldogs in Lebanon 2–0, but on the road Cumberland lost to Vanderbilt 60–0; South Carolina 68–0; and to the University of Tennessee in Knoxville 101–0. Cumberland played Tennessee one other time, in 1897 as the Vols squeaked by 6–0.

Cumberland in the early days did tackle a number of schools which now are members of the Southeastern Conference. In 1903 Cumberland beat Alabama 44–0, LSU 41–0, Vanderbilt 6–0, and tied Clemson 11–11 in a bowl game.

It was but fifty minutes by rail from Lebanon to Nashville. The route from there would turn south to Birmingham, Alabama, and then due east for Atlanta.

Many on the train had been present at Horn Springs the night before, and many of them were nursing headaches and hangovers. George was grateful for the quiet time. He had enjoyed the hoopla of the party but had abstained from the alcoholic drinks.

The gentle rocking motion of the train, swaying back and forth, combined with the clickity-clink rhythm of the wheels on the track made for an inviting lullaby that led to a slumber much deeper than napping. George was soon in dreamland, making up lost time for the sleep he had been deprived of over the past week.

As the train drew near to Birmingham, some of the Cumberland entourage reflected on the school's glory days when they played the University of Alabama. By jingo, last year they had even matched up with the University of Tennessee.

As a few of the groggy athletes began to stir from their sleep, one could hear voices asking, "Where are we?" and "Are we there yet?"

The scenery was spectacular as the train crossed rolling hills leading into and out of small towns and past farm fields blanketed white with acres and acres of cotton bolls ripe for picking.

A happy voice from the back of the car hollered, "'Bout time for a beer!"

The frivolity began with beer, sandwiches, and pretzels and gathered speed with music via musicians with a guitar, fiddle and harmonica. There was dancing in the aisles.

George's first thought was to quiet them down, but then he reasoned to himself, "Oh, let them have their fun. It wasn't going to matter one whit of difference as to the outcome of the game. He knew they were like lambs being led to the slaughter, and he knew that he was responsible for the situation. He rationalized it was best that they enjoy themselves today, and tomorrow would take care of itself. He did not wish for his mind to linger on that scenario.

At about six o'clock the lights of Atlanta could be seen as the train approached from the northwest. The conductor alerted the riders, "We're only about 20 miles out."

That was his signal to his somewhat rowdy passengers that it was time for them to sober up, and collect their belongings. His announcement received cheers of joy from the unsuspecting lambs.

The Bulldog squad

George counted himself fortunate to have a final roster of 15 players, all Cumberland students except for a reporter, George Geiger, whom he had picked up from The Nashville Tennessean. One Cumberland athlete, Pete Gray, had actually played college football for a short while in Oklahoma.

The squad was dominated by members of the Kappa Sigma fraternity.

The Cumberland team and their respective hometowns were: T.N. (Morris) Gouger, Robstown, Texas; E.L. (Leon) McDonald, Bay City, Texas; G.T. (George) Murphy, Huntingdon, Tenn.; C.E. (Eddie) Edwards, Savannah, Ga.; C.W. (Charlie) Warwick, West Palm Beach, Fla.; D.R. (Dow) Cope, Yakima, Wash.; Gentry Dugat, Beeville, Texas; D.N. (David) Harsh, Gallatin, Tenn.; E.W. McCall, Hamshire, Texas; H.F. Carney, Cheatham County, Tenn.; R.E. (Pete) Gray, Fairfax, Okla.; B.F. (Bird) Patey, Tullahoma, Tenn.; J.D. (Dean) Gauldin, Dallas, Texas; P.V. (Porter) Hamblen, Mt. Juliet, Tenn.; and George Geiger, Nashville, Tenn. The coach was Ernest (Butch) McQueen of Lebanon, Tenn., and the manager was G.E. (George) Allen of Baldwyn, Miss.

Although formally listed as team manager, George also threw himself as a part of the Cumberland squad playing intermittently at fullback.

TERMINAL STATION

This train depot opened in 1905 and was the larger of two rail stations in downtown Atlanta during the period. Union Station was the other. Served by Southern Railway, Seaboard Railroad, Central of Georgia, and the Atlanta and West Point, Terminal Station was convenient to downtown Atlanta hotels, the business district and other places of interests. The Atlanta Convention Bureau marketed Terminal Station as "the gateway to sunshine" because it was the center point in the southeast where many rail travelers from northern states in the fall and winter months would change trains on their way to the warmer climates of Florida and the Gulf Coast. Terminal Station survived long enough to see one refurbishing project in 1947 but closed in 1970 and was demolished two years later.

Terminal Station

As the train pulled into Terminal Station in downtown Atlanta, the shouting and cheering became louder. The decibel level inside the car was so high that the squealing of the iron wheels rubbing against the rails as the engineer applied the brakes couldn't be heard.

Waiting for Cumberland's arrival was a delegation from Georgia Tech. President Kenneth Matheson and Coach John Heisman were not among the greeters.

Patiently the group from the host school waited as the Cumberland players and their fellow passengers gathered their suitcases and burlap potato sacks. Once together with all their apparatus they stood in four uneven ranks. Despite the gentlemen

wearing neckties and three-piece suits and the women adorned in
long skirts, the group appeared unkempt and out-of-sorts.

George stood before his rumpled platoon and barked simple
instructions.

"We're going to follow our genial hosts down the avenue a
few blocks to the Georgian Terrace Hotel. The school has taken
care of the team's rooms, but the others of you are on your own.

"Tomorrow is going to be a long day. I want you players
to get a good meal tonight at the hotel. Turn in early. Get a
good night's sleep, and be downstairs for breakfast at eight
o'clock sharp.

"We'll go over our plans for the game after supper,"
he ended.

The Cumberland corps marched down the metropolitan
sidewalk lit by gas lamps and ogled their surroundings. They were
mesmerized.

Young George Allen, 20, mentor, father figure and disciplinarian, reckoned that despite his best efforts the words he had
uttered likely had fallen on deaf ears. This bunch had not come
to Atlanta to eat and sleep. He was just prayerful that all fifteen
would show for breakfast before the drive to Grant Field.

CHAPTER
NINE

GAME DAY
ARRIVES

Reporting for breakfast

One by one they came straggling in.

It was not a pretty sight, but they reported for breakfast as George had requested.

Heads bowed, eyes half shuttered, these guys, Cumberland's football team for the day, didn't appear in the least to be eligible to be on the stage against a Georgia Tech team playing for a national title.

They were hung-over from a long night of partying, had gotten only a couple of hours of sleep, and in a few hours would be facing their very own Goliath.

There was not much chatter at breakfast. There was muttering about passing the eggs, jam for the hotel's famously held homemade biscuits and calls all across the dining room for Bayer aspirin, a product introduced in 1899 to help relieve headaches. Many listed on George's roster were suffering from lingering hangover headaches contracted the night before from the consumption of too much of Atlanta's best libations.

As the table was being cleared, George stood with clip board in hand and began making announcements.

"Georgia Tech will send transportation to pick us up at 1 o'clock. You and your equipment bags (potato sacks) should be waiting at the sidewalk in front of the hotel at that time. Do not be late. Grant Field is a few miles east of here and it's a long walk.

"The game is scheduled to start at three. Drink lots of coffee, water and juice and try to get yourselves sober and ready as best you can. I will see you in front of the hotel in about three hours. Again, let me remind you, do not be late," said George as he closed in his most persuasive commanding tone.

On the Georgia Tech campus Coach Heisman was taking care of business.

His players assembled for breakfast at six-thirty. They were not hung-over. Their eyes were not bloodshot. And they had reported to Coach Heisman, as instructed, following a full eight hours of sleep.

Honey-smothered buttermilk biscuits, fruit (with an emphasis on bananas for potassium), eggs, beefsteaks, bottomless glasses of freshly squeezed orange juice, an assortment of nuts and pastries, and a generous portion of sliced Georgia peaches for good measure comprised the Tech breakfast menu.

Coach Heisman prepared the same for this game as he did every game. He didn't give a hoot in hell as to whether or not Cumberland fielded a genuine football team. But he did know the caliber of his athletes and that they were ready.

He preached his axioms for success on the gridiron to an attentive audience. He warned them about the possible what-ifs and trick plays. And he recanted to his players the events of the previous spring when Cumberland had humiliated his Georgia Tech baseball team.

John Heisman was not about to let a championship season slip through his hands because he was not prepared. He expected to win this game in a big way.

Those who played for Coach Heisman recognized him as a strict disciplinarian and a man who had strong objections to profanity and fumbling. He admonished his teams to play as hard on the practice field as they would on a game field.

His pre-game and halftime motivational talks were as natural to him as a politician speaking on the courthouse steps. He had trained as an actor. For years Heisman spent his summers working as an aspiring actor focusing his energies on plays by Shakespeare.

Among other peculiarities, he would make his athletes take cold showers after long practice sessions and rewarded them with hot water after a winning game day.

A Nice Day

More than an hour before the kickoff the first of what would amount to several hundred spectators began to arrive at Grant Field. The vast majority were Georgia Tech supporters. The only folks sitting in the bleachers cheering for Cumberland were the seventy-five or so who had accompanied the team on the train.

On this typical Georgia day in October, the temperature was expected to reach the mid-70s by early afternoon. A little breeze provided brief wisps of relief, as there was still plenty of humidity in the air. It was going to be a long, hot afternoon for players on both sides of the line of scrimmage.

Cumberland's tiny platoon was about to undergo an afternoon engagement that would prove to be a grueling experience for two reasons. First, the night of revelry and lack of sleep had sapped their energy, and second, a Georgia Tech team, overwhelming in size and strength, was determined to wreak havoc on the school that had victimized their coach six months ago on the Cumberland baseball diamond.

Grant Field 1913

GRANT FIELD

The area known today as Grant Field was leased for seven years, beginning in 1904, before it was acquired and became Georgia Tech's permanent football home. Located on the Tech campus, in its early days Grant Field proved an inadequate venue for college football.

The tract, known as "The Flats," was uneven and peppered with rocks, and there was no place for fans to watch games except to stand along the sidelines. Coach Heisman had encouraged Tech's Athletic Association to lease the area from the E.C. Peters Land Company. The field was renovated in 1905 when Tech students and alumni and Atlanta residents erected the first stands adjacent to the field.

In 1906 Tech received a $17,500 grant from the Georgia state legislature to enlarge the campus. Proceeds were used to purchase the tract of land that the school had been leasing for use as an athletic field.

In 1913 a $15,000 donation was made by John W. Grant to the university in memory of his deceased son, Hugh Inman Grant. These funds helped construct permanent concrete grandstands on the field's west side. The next year Grant made a second donation to Tech. This $20,000 was used to expand the concrete bleacher seating.

On November 18, 1916, before the kickoff of a game between Tech and Georgia, the gridiron was officially named Hugh Inman Grant Field.

Continued

In 1920 John Grant, then a member of the Georgia Tech Board of Trustees, made a third contribution of $50,000 to enable the university to complete the purchase on the entire tract of land comprising the area in which Grant Field is located.

The concrete stands on the east side of Grant Field were added in 1921. After several subsequent expansions, by the early 2000s, the site now known as Bobby Dodd Stadium at Grant Field seated more than 55,000.

Donned in colors of black and gold, a growing legion of Georgia Tech fans was entering the stadium. Most of the men were sporting high-collar white and pinstriped dress shirts and three-piece suits coordinated with colorful neck ties. The fashion for women of the day was long skirts, lightweight jackets, and large, broad brim hats.

George began to feel sick in the pit of his stomach. His mind was scrambling as he tried to come up with the right words of encouragement for his team before it trotted on to the field. Only one thought registered in his head. Those final words issued by Coach Heisman after the baseball loss game: "I will get revenge."

As game time grew nearer, Grant Field swelled to capacity with a crowd of more than 1,000.

The city of Atlanta was primed for this bout, as for weeks Heisman had been delivering blistering verbal attacks against the Bulldogs, preaching how the small Tennessee university had not played the baseball game honorably back in the spring. He was convinced that Cumberland had filled their roster with semi-pro players from Nashville.

"They were not students," Heisman declared to anyone who would listen. "They were grown men who had been playing baseball for years and were being paid for their abilities. They were professionals."

For some time before the day of this match, his indictment of Cumberland had been printed in Atlanta newspapers as well as papers across the country. His charge against Cumberland had been used as a rallying cry for today's game, all a small part of Heisman's master plan to grab the national championship.

Because of the hype engulfing the game and the magnitude of Heisman's reputation, the gridiron duel was covered by dozens of newspapers, while the results would be filed across the nation by reporters for the Associated Press and United Press Associations (later United Press International).

Among the sports scribes covering the game was Grantland Rice, working at the time for The New York Tribune. A personal friend of the famed coach, Rice began following Heisman with his "sporting news" reports early in the coach's career. The two collaborated to write "Understand Football," first published in 1929.

Pregame team messages

George Allen and his counterpart John Heisman found it difficult to deliver the appropriate pre-game message to their squads.

In opposite end zones the men fumbled for the exact words to express their concerns for the match up.

Heisman wondered if George had again stacked the deck against him by bringing in a bunch of ringers from other schools or possibly even semi-pro players.

And George didn't know to what degree Coach Heisman would make good on his promise for revenge. Could some his players, his frat brothers, get crippled? What was the worst that could happen?

GRANTLAND RICE

Born in Murfreesboro, Tennessee, the famed writer stood six-feet-and-two-inches tall when he played football and baseball at Vanderbilt University where he served as captain of the Vandy nine his senior year. In the classroom he excelled in writing and preferred  courses in English, literature, Latin and Greek and he graduated as a Phi Beta Kappa member.

In 1901 Rice began his career in sports writing with The Nashville Daily News, and a year later was hired as sports editor for The Atlanta Journal. He held a sports writing post with The Nashville Tennessean after his marriage in 1906, and then answered a call to write for the New York Evening Mail in 1910. His columns became a popular regiment for New York readers, and in 1914 The New York Tribune published a full page advertisement welcoming him to its staff.

After a stint in the Army during World War I Rice returned to New York in 1919 and continued his career in journalism. In 1922 Rice became the first person to call a live radio baseball play-by-play broadcast when he sat behind the microphone for the World Series.

Rice, whose sports column became syndicated and appeared in as many as 100 newspapers, also edited American Golfer magazine,

Continued

authored books and poems, and wrote articles for Collier's and Look magazines. In 1925 he succeeded Walter Camp in selecting the annual All-America football team.

Of his works, he has been quoted most for these words: "For when the one Great Scorer comes to write against your name, He marks—not that you won or lost—but how you played the game."

Grantland Rice died of a heart attack at age 73 on July 14, 1954, in his New York City office after completing a column about Willie Mays and the 1954 All-Star game, one of more than 22,000 columns he wrote during his career.

Certainly Coach Heisman's pep talk would be the easier of the two.

The stoic coach, age 47, began his address, saying, "Men, you likely believe this Cumberland University team will be a pushover, but let me remind you that it was not that many years ago that this school competed head to head with some of the finest team's in the nation.

"They do not appear to have many talented players, and their equipment looks to be hand-me-downs, but looks can be deceiving. Go out there and hit them hard. Play your best. Be watchful and alert. Never quit. We have a national championship to win, but we must win this game first."

Heisman ended his speech and then he and his team sprinted to its place on the sidelines near the 50-yard line.

Meanwhile, George was trying to pull together a few sentences himself. Unlike his masterful foe, George had never delivered a pre-game message, not at least for a game of this magnitude. The closest he had come to anything of this nature was perhaps a closing argument in a moot court proceeding.

"Fellows, I'm not sure where to begin, but let me assure you that your commitment today will be recorded and long remembered," said the student manager.

"Tech is playing this game to stay in the hunt for a national championship. You've volunteered for this game to win the hearts of students back home and hundreds of alumni who love Cumberland University. Despite the outcome of this contest, I promise that history will view each of you as winners and champions.

"The men we're facing do this every day. They are big, fast and tough. Their coach has them revved tighter than a Chevy 490. And because of the trick I pulled last spring, Coach Heisman is going to do his best to beat the absolute hell out of us. If I could make that baseball game go away, I would. But I can't turn back the clock. That one is on me, and frankly that has a lot to do with why you're here today.

GEORGIA RIVALRY

Clean, old-fashioned hate is the title that has been applied to the football rivalry between the University of Georgia and Georgia Tech. The two first met on the gridiron in 1893. Tech holds the record for the longest winning streak by taking eight consecutive games from 1949 to 1956. However, through the end of the 2014 season, Georgia had compiled the best record at 64–40–5.

"Go out there. Play well. Enjoy the moment and don't take any chances. Remember all we want to do today is play this game and get back to good ole Lebanon, Tennessee, and our dear Cumberland campus in one piece. Good luck."

The coin toss

George sent his reliable friend Gentry Dugat to the center of the field for the coin toss. Greeting Dugat from the Tech bench was "Froggie" Morrison, the Engineers star quarterback.

STAR ATHLETE: *Douglas Eaton "Froggie" Morrison, a native of Dade County, Georgia, was one of Georgia Tech's outstanding athletes. Excelling in football as a running back and quarterback, he also played catcher on Tech's baseball team. He received numerous honors for his football talents including being voted to the All Southern team in 1915 but may best be remembered as the quarterback of the 1916 Engineers team that defeated Cumberland 222–0. After graduating from Tech the young athlete entered the Army and served in World War I. When his service was completed, he returned to Georgia where in 1933 he accepted an assistant coaching position at Tech. Born in 1893, Morrison died in 1973.*

Morrison called "heads," and the referee flipped a Liberty half dollar four feet into the air and they watched it land on the green turf.

Heads it was. Tech chose to kick off.

The team captains shook hands, exchanged best wishes, and Morrison sprinted to his sideline with an excited grin scrolled across his face. He and his accompanying 37 comrades were eager for the battle to begin. They would boot the ball toward the south end zone.

Dugat trotted casually back to his team and reported that Cumberland would be receiving the ball and have the first opportunity to score.

Tech's starting line-up

The starting team for Georgia Tech included Jim Senter, Chitwood, Virginia; W.G. Carpenter, Newnan, Georgia; Bob Long, Atlanta, Georgia; G.M. (Pup) Phillips, Carnesville, Georgia; G.R. (Hip) West, Chattanooga, Tennessee; J.C. (Canty) Alexander, Spartanburg, South Carolina; R.S. (Si) Bell, Atlanta, Georgia; D.E. (Froggie) Morrison, Trenton, Georgia; Strup Strupper, Atlanta, Georgia; J.T. Talley Johnston, Chattanooga, Tennessee; and T.L. Tommy Spence, Thomasville, Georgia.

Other prominent players on the squad were Marshall Guill, Sparta, Georgia; Albert Hill, Washington, Georgia; Bill Fincher, Spring Place, Georgia; Jim Preas, Johnson City, Tennessee; Bud Shaver, Dayton, Georgia; John Mangham, Stone Mountain, Georgia; Wally Smith, Atlanta, Georgia; Dawson Teague, Augusta,

Tech's 1916 team

THREE OFFICIALS

During this period of football, game officiating was left to three men, an umpire, head linesman and referee. The referee had responsibilities requiring him to notify each team of penalties and other communications, explaining penalties to the offending team captain and coach, overseeing the application of first-down measurements and other matters.

The referee was positioned in the backfield of the team on offense usually about ten yards or less behind the quarterback. The referee was charged with making the final decision in the event of a disagreement concerning the rules of play.

The umpire's duties included enforcing the rules of play, but he was also the one responsible for recording the score, the number of time-outs used by each team, and he was also the one who conducted the coin toss to determine who would kick off.

The head linesman was positioned near the line of scrimmage and was to watch for offside violations, encroachments by linemen and other wrongs that might occur near the line of scrimmage.

Georgia; Curtis McRae, Norfolk, Virginia; George C. Griffin, Savannah, Georgia; and A.B. Hill, Harlan, Kentucky.

Tech substitutes included H.R. Dunwoody; P.O. (Frank) Pruitt, Thomaston, Georgia; A.R. (Alton) Colcord, Atlanta, Georgia; S.O. (Samuel) Fitzgerald; J.C. (Julian) Hightower; Ralph Puckett,

Tifton, Georgia; Hugh Mauck, Ft. Meyers, Florida; W.F. Thweatt; W.C. Mathis; J.C. Funkhouser, Hillsborough, New Jersey; Bill Ward; C.F. (Charlie) Turner; J.W. (Wright) Brown; Stan Fellers, Rome, Georgia; W.F. (Bill) Simpson, Atlanta, Georgia; R.G. (Bob) Glover; and G.E. (George) Ansley.

The Cumberland team positioned itself to receive the game's first kickoff.

Standing near the middle of the field, the game referee blew his whistle signaling the game had begun.

CHAPTER
TEN

THE BIG
GAME

Cumberland receives first kick

Jim Preas of Johnson City, Tennessee, booms the opening kick to the 25-yard line where the Cumberland runner downs the ball immediately, not even attempting to run with the pigskin.

> JIM PREAS earned his degree from Georgia Tech and shortly after graduating accepted a head coaching job at The Newport News Apprentice School in Newport News, Va. for three seasons from 1919 to 1921 establishing a better than 80 percent winning record at 18–3–1. After his coaching stint he returned to his native Johnson City where he became a successful businessman, civic leader, and was elected to the city commission.

On the first play of the game Morris Gouger runs to a small opening off left tackle for a gain of three yards. Not a bad beginning for the Bulldogs, clad in maroon jerseys.

On second down Leon McDonald plows headlong into the heart of a beefy Tech line for no gain

Cumberland elects to punt on third down. McDonald boots a 20-yard punt to Preas, who returns the kick 18 yards and sets Georgia Tech up for its first score at the Cumberland 20-yard line.

Everett Strup Strupper

(Cumberland's first running play, based on statistics in the record book, proved Grantland Rice wrong in his report of the game when he claimed "Cumberland's greatest individual play of the game occurred when fullback Allen circled right end for a 6-yard loss." The fullback in this instance was none other than George Allen himself. He inserted himself in and out of the line-up throughout the

ALABAMA'S RED ELEPHANT

George Everett "Strup" Strupper Jr., a half-back from Columbus, Georgia, was named a consensus All-American on Heisman's 1917 national championship team. After graduating from Tech he became an assistant football coach at Mercer for a short while and then made a career in sports writing at The Atlanta Journal. Strupper is credited with creating the red elephant mascot for the University of Alabama in an article he wrote on October 8, 1930 for the paper following an Alabama-Mississippi game in which he referred to Alabama's lineman as "red elephants" because of their size and strength and the crimson jerseys they wore. Strupper died in 1950 at age 57 and was posthumously elected to the College Football Hall of Fame in 1972.

afternoon. Reliving the game later in life when speaking at public events Allen would often lament about Rice's report on his effort.)

In possession of the ball for the first time, Coach Heisman orders a running play around left end. George Everett "Strup" Strupper scampers 20 yards into the end zone and scores the game's first touchdown on Tech's first offensive play. Preas kicks his first extra point of the afternoon, and Tech leads 7–0.

The second kickoff

Coach Heisman instructs Tommy Spence to airmail Tech's second kickoff following the Engineers' score. Cumberland's Morris Gouger catches the ball near the 5-yard line, advancing the ball only five more yards before being swarmed by a platoon of Tech players.

MORRIS GOUGER made his way to Cumberland from Robstown, Texas. He earned a degree from the Cumberland Law School, returned to his hometown and later became president of the National Bank of Robstown.

DAVID NEWBY (NATHAN) HARSH graduated from the Cumberland Law School and joined the Army serving as an officer in World War I. From Gallatin, Tennessee, a community about 19 miles northwest of Lebanon, Harsh returned after the war to practice law and later moved to Memphis where he became chairman of the Shelby County (Memphis, Tennessee) Governing Board and Board of Adjustments. He served in that position from 1936 to 1954.

LEON McDONALD, from Bay City, Texas, was also a law school student at Cumberland in 1916. He and Gouger are remembered for perhaps the most notable verbal exchange between two Cumberland players in the game. McDonald took a botched snap from the center fumbled the football toward Gouger. He supposedly yelled to Gouger "pick the ball up," and Gouger, eyeballing an army of Tech lineman pouring in his direction, shouted back, "Pick it up yourself. It's your fumble."

Game day action

With the ball resting on the 10-yard line, Cumberland's C.E. (Eddie) Murphy gets the call for a running sweep around right end. He fumbles the ball, and Tech's Guill recovers and rambles to the end zone for Tech's second TD.

Preas follows up with the extra point conversion and Tech takes control quickly with a lead of 14–0.

On the ensuing kickoff Preas kicks the ball to Gouger, who makes one of the biggest gains for the Tennessee school, returning the ball 20 yards to the 30-yard line.

On the first play from scrimmage on this possession Cumberland quarterback Leon McDonald fumbles, and George "Hip" West recovers for Tech.

GEORGE "HIP" WEST *graduated from Georgia Tech, played right guard for Coach Heisman's Golden Tornadoes from 1915–1917 and received a degree in medicine from Emory University School of Medicine. He returned home to Chattanooga, Tennessee, and became a prominent surgeon.*

Georgia Tech's offense returns to the field. Strup Strupper takes the hand-off from quarterback Froggie Morrison and dashes 15 yards around right end, making it second down on the Cumberland 5-yard line. Preas continues the offensive attack, running the ball into the end zone and scoring the Engineers' third touchdown. Preas converts the extra point kick and now the score is 21–0.

A bit more than only five minutes into the game, and Tech has secured a commanding lead. The home fans are jubilant, and Heisman's warning to his players seems to have been unfounded.

Kicking off for a fourth time, Preas sends it to the 10-yard line, and McDonald advances the ball for the Bulldogs to the Cumberland 20.

Gouger runs on first down and loses five yards.

The Bulldogs then option to go with two pass plays. Quarterback McDonald fails to connect with his receivers,

Tech players tackle Cumberland running back

and he punts on fourth down. His kick travels only 20 yards, bounces a couple of times and lands out-of-bounds. Georgia Tech takes over on the Cumberland 35.

A Tech substitute, Theodore "Buzz" Shaver, playing fullback, strikes around left end for 25 yards. On the following next play Strupper hits the same hole and scores from 10 yards out. Preas kicks the extra point. Tech has a 28–0 advantage.

On Cumberland's sideline George Allen begins to panic. He's concerned not so much about the score as he is about the health of his team. He fears a serious injury could be inflicted on any of his men on any given play whether Cumberland is on defense or offense.

He summons his team to the sideline for a brief pow wow as Tech gathers for a fifth kickoff.

"This is not going well, to say the least. Let's take it one play at a time. Keep your chins up and eyes open. We all want to get out of here in one piece."

This time instead of receiving the kick, Allen decides to take a different route.

This era of college football allowed the team that had been scored upon the option to either receive the next kickoff or to go on defense and kick to its opponent. George chooses to kick the ball to Tech.

Heisman, somewhat surprised by the tactic, ponders to himself, "Why would Cumberland, down by four touchdowns, want to kick instead of receive?"

For the first time in the game, the great coach sends his kick return team on to the gridiron.

McDonald, Cumberland's go-to-guy, delivers a strong kick to the Tech 20-yard line where Buzz Shaver catches the ball and flashes 70 yards to the Cumberland 10.

Cumberland's defense, already weary, allows Strupper a 9-yard plunge. J.C. "Canty" Alexander then takes it the final yard for the TD. Preas kicks the ball between the uprights, and Heisman's squad is in front by 35 points.

While Allen's decision to kick off instead of receive didn't yield any better results for his team, he sticks with the strategy, instructing McDonald to kick again.

McDonald boots it to the 35 where W.G. "Six" Carpenter cradles the ball and returns it five yards. From the 40-yard line Strupper bolts through the Cumberland defense and runs 60 yards for another score. Preas converts the extra point, and the scoreboard reads 42–0.

WALTER G. "SIX" CARPENTER, from Newnan, *Georgia, was a captain on the Georgia Tech national championship team of 1917. He was voted All-America and All-Southern honors and made a member of the Georgia Tech Football Hall of Fame. Tech's Golden Tornadoes went 9–0 in 1917 and outscored their opponents 491–17 to claim their championship.*

Following orders from Allen, McDonald kicks the ball for a third time following the Tech score. This kickoff sails to Tech's 25 where Alexander catches it on the fly and takes it to the 35-yard line. Shaver gets the first call from scrimmage and rips off 25 yards around right end. Then Ralph Puckett grinds his way up the middle for 5 yards. Fullback Tommy Spence polishes off the drive, carrying the ball into the end zone from 35 yards out. Preas kicks the extra point, and the lead rises to 49–0.

George decides it's time to receive again. Tommy Spence kicks off, and McDonald catches the ball on the Cumberland 10, stumbles and is tackled immediately. He throws two incomplete passes and punts on third down. Strupper catches the ball and sprints 45 yards for a touchdown. After another Preas kick, Tech notches its 56th point.

Cumberland's McDonald kicks off once again. This time it's a dandy, his best of the day. But despite his best effort Tech's Spence fields the ball on the 10 and races 90 yards for a touchdown. Preas sends the ball through the uprights, and seven more points are tacked on to the scoreboard.

On the final series of the first quarter Cumberland sets up shop for its offense at its own 25-yard line after Gouger returns a Tommy Spence kick 10 yards. On first down Gouger runs the ball for a five-yard loss. McDonald follows suit. Facing a third down and 20, McDonald hurls an incomplete pass. The first quarter is over, but the massacre has just begun.

Reviewing the first quarter

In the first quarter Tech scored 63 unanswered points on nine touchdown runs and six Preas extra-points. The Tornadoes gained 163 yards on runs, and 180 yards on kickoff returns.

For the day Tech averaged scoring 3.8 points per minute.

JOHN HEISMAN'S ESSENTIALS

Always
Always play with your head
Always listen for the signal
Always block your opponent at any cost
Always start as fast as you can
Always be where the ball is
Always win the game

Don't
Don't lose your head
Don't fumble the ball
Don't tackle high
Don't stop running because you are behind
Don't hesitate about falling on the ball
Don't let a runner escape you after you have him
Don't lose the game

Can't
You can't play football without brains
You can't play too aggressively
You can't afford to waste time talking
You can't play ball with a swelled head
You can't win without using these principles

Never
Never drop the ball
Never get excited
Never give up
Never forget that a football player may be a gentleman

No rest for the wary

Cumberland players had been scrambling for their lives for the first 15 minutes of the game. They were battered, bruised and pooped and still had three more quarters to play.

Grateful for the respite, they knelt briefly on the sideline where their leader tried to soothe them as best he could.

"Fellows, we've got three quarters left, just 45 minutes. You can do it. I know you can. Hang in there. Next time you come to the sidelines the game will be half over and you can rest for 20 minutes," he said, feeling guilty.

Across the field Heisman continued to caution his team, while behind his back his players were rolling their eyes with an "I can't believe he's telling us this horse dump" attitude. They already knew this game was in the bag, and those poor guys from Cumberland were hapless, without a prayer in the world of mounting any form of a threatening comeback.

The Tech offensive attack resembled a giant bowling ball tumbling off of Stone Mountain. Nothing was going to stop them.

Heisman told his men to pass no heed to the scoreboard, to keep playing full speed ahead until they heard the whistle. And reminded them constantly of his essential guidelines of winning football.

The second quarter began with Cumberland facing a fourth down on its 5-yard line. McDonald punted the ball 50 yards to Charlie Turner, a back-up Tech running back, who ran back the kick 45 yards to the Cumberland 20. On the first play off left end Jim Senter took the ball into the end zone. Another extra point off the toes of Preas ups the score to 70–0.

Tech kicks off with the ball falling into the hands of George Murphy, who runs 15 yards to the Cumberland 35 yard line. On first and ten, Gouger gains five yards on a play off right tackle, and McDonald follows with a completed pass for four more yards. On third and one, McDonald punts but the pigskin slices off his foot and angles out of bounds 11 yards beyond the line of scrimmage.

Tech's Senter races around end for 40 yards before a Bulldog brings him down on the 15. Preas sprints the remainder of the way for the TD and caps off the drive with an extra point.

The guys posting the score with wooden numbered plaques shake their heads and position two plaques displaying the number 77 in the Georgia Tech slot.

Preas kicks off and Gouger returns the ball five yards to the 20. McDonald attempts a pass but Tech's Marshall Guill intercepts and scores. Another extra point is added and the score mounts to 84–0.

TOMMY SPENCE *was an outstanding Tech athlete. He was voted All-Southern for his skill set on the football field but also played baseball, basketball and ran track. Spence, who enlisted in the Army after his time at Georgia Tech, was killed in France in 1918 at age 22, two years after the game with Cumberland.*

MARSHALL GUILL, *although a kicker in the 1916 Cumberland game, became one of John Heisman's most prominent quarterbacks three years later in 1919 for Georgia Tech's Golden Tornado, a name given Tech teams between 1917 and 1929. Guill also played end. He earned a degree in mechanical engineering and was killed in a car accident near Guilford, Conn. At the age of 33.*

BILL FINCHER *besides having kicking duties was an outstanding tackle for Tech. During his college career he was voted a consensus All-America and All-Southern and later was named to the Tech All-Era Team. In 1974 he was inducted into the College Football Hall of Fame. Fincher had a glass eye. It's said that from time to time when a game got tough in the trenches he'd pull his glass piece from his eye as if an opponent had knocked it out and would then warn his foe, "So that's how you want to play."*

ALL AMERICAN
1920
Ga Tech Tackle
World Champion Goal
Kicker
65 out of 68
attempts

Bill
Fincher

Tech kicker Bill Fincher

The Cumberland athletes appear to be lost souls stumbling through a desert. Their jerseys are soaked in sweat. The water boy on the sidelines has already refilled the water bucket four times.

Meanwhile Heisman is substituting four or five players after every play. His squad stays fresh and alert. Jealously, George eyes the army across the way and then looks bleakly at his bench where three Bulldogs sit with their heads hanging down.

The next few possessions produce quick scores for Tech.

Preas continues to boom long kicks deep into Cumberland territory. Murphy snares his next missile and falls on the 10. Eddie Edwards takes the ball on first and ten and fumbles. Bob Glover recovers for Tech, and George Griffin scores for Tech from the 10. The score goes to 91–0.

On the next kickoff, Murphy runs five yards to the Cumberland 15. McDonald heaves a pass only to have it intercepted by Senter, who takes it to the three. Strupper scores on first down, and Tech has now amassed 98 points.

Preas' next kickoff zooms out of bounds on the Cumberland 10. McDonald runs the ball up the middle for no gain. On second down and ten, he punts. The 15-yard kick is taken by Guill, and he hustles with it for 10 yards before he is tackled on the Cumberland 15. George Griffin carries the ball twice before Bob Glover hits pay dirt in the end zone. The score is 105–0.

Morris Gouger takes the Preas kickoff for Cumberland returning the ball to the 10-yard line. On the first play from scrimmage, Gouger fumbles. Preas, a one-man wrecking crew, recovers the ball, runs it into the end zone and kicks the extra point. Tech leads 112–0.

George Murphy receives the kickoff and takes it to the Cumberland 15. Murphy, relieving McDonald at quarterbacking, throws a pass that is intercepted by Stan Fellers. Fellers returns it 17 yards for a touchdown. After another Preas kick, Tech widens the gap to 119–0.

Again Murphy takes the kickoff and advances 10 yards to the Cumberland 25. On this sequence Murphy loses two yards and McDonald loses five yards on consecutive plays and then McDonald punts on fourth down. Fellers catches McDonald's 20-yard punt and returns it 33 yards for the final score of the first half. Preas makes good the extra point, and Tech leads 126–0.

Murphy returns the ensuing kickoff 15 yards to the 15, and the referee's whistle signals the end to the first half.

Halftime

The 14 bruised and battered Cumberland boys limped to their end zone and fell out on the turf. Their bodies and psyches were sapped, and worst of all the game was but half over.

Tech managed to double its margin in the second quarter, scoring nine touchdowns and nine extra points exactly as it had done in the first period.

While Heisman had substituted frequently, the scoring and key plays were carried out by a handful of trusty Tech players.

If there was any glimmer of excellence for Cumberland, it had to be McDonald, the Texas law student, who handled the kicking chores. At the beginning of the second quarter he booted his longest punt, a 50-yarder.

For Cumberland the break between halves was a godsend. Several players soaked wounds with hydro-peroxide, others sucked down water served from glass milk bottles, and some sat gazing into the sky dreaming about when this nightmare would be over.

There was no peace in the Georgia Tech end zone.

Coach Heisman had conferred with his assistants about what miscues they had observed in the first half before addressing his team.

HALFTIME

Teams during this early period of the game did not retreat to a dressing room for the respite at halftime. Instead, they gathered in their respective end zone, drank water, kneeled on one knee, and took instructions from their coach.

The athletes had learned to expect to hear the worst from their coach at the half. But the circumstances today were somewhat different.

The team had played about as perfect a game as they could. Cumberland had never crossed the 50-yard line into Tech territory. Surely, thought the squad, their coach has to be pleased.

"Gather 'round men," said Coach Heisman. "We have a great task before us today. We are on a track to win a national title, but cannot succeed until we win this game today.

"We must continue to focus our attention on our opponent. We cannot afford to be complacent. We must be vigilant. There are still 30 minutes of play remaining in this contest, and we are not about to retreat."

Just before his team takes the field for the second half, Heisman offer words of encouragement.

"You're doing fine, men. But you just can't tell what those Cumberland players have up their sleeves. They may spring a surprise. Be alert! Hit 'em clean, but hit 'em hard. Hard!"

One hundred yards away George Allen is coercing his players to get off the ground and be mentally prepared for one more half.

He has a secret which he is not yet ready to spill.

George leaves his team and walks briskly almost sprinting to the referees just before they are ready to signal the teams for the start of second half. In a humble and respectful tone he asks to have a word with the trio before they whistle for the kickoff.

Tech's Joe Guyon

The three agree to listen.

George inquires in his best moot court demeanor as to whether they would consider reducing the length of the third and fourth quarters from 15 minutes to 12-and-a-half minutes.

"There is no way we can win this game. We're getting the bejeezus whomped out of us. Can you have a little mercy? The crowd's gotten what they want. Coach Heisman has gotten what he wants. And we just want to get out of here in one piece and back home to Lebanon, Tennessee," reasoned George, taking a page from his contract law textbook where it is understood that if a transaction is fair for both parties and both parties are good with their contractual obligations then it must be a good contract.

The head referee hesitated but offered hope. He told George he understood the request but allowed that Coach Heisman would have to agree before the proposition could be administered.

Heisman observed this curious conversation from across the field. Immediately, he suspected that George was plotting some sort of trickery to give Cumberland an advantage in the second half just as he had warned his players.

When the referee reached him, Heisman uttered the first words.

"You don't know the man with whom you are dealing. He is not trustworthy and whatever he may have told you or plotted will be stained with deceit. For that I can be certain."

The coaching legend was still fuming from the 22–0 loss to Cumberland in baseball last spring.

Heisman ranted on and referred to the fiasco on the ball diamond until the ref raised his hand as if stopping traffic on Peachtree Avenue and said "enough."

He explained that Cumberland simply made a request to shorten the game.

"Coach Heisman, are you OK with 12-and-one-half-minute quarters for the second half?" the ref asked.

Heisman nodded affirmatively, and the deal was done.

CHAPTER
ELEVEN

THE SCORE
ESCALATES

The second half

Trailing 126–0 to begin the third quarter and with the option to kick or receive, Cumberland chooses to receive.

Any visions Allen and his team might have had back at the celebration at Horn Springs in Tennessee a week ago about upstaging Georgia Tech had by now been transformed into a nightmare.

Some three decades following the game Allen in an autobiography confessed that he actually thought the team he had put together to play Tech "looked pretty hot" and had a decent chance to win the game.

But his vision proved blurred.

By now the Bulldogs each were just prayerful that they would survive the remaining 25 minutes of play.

Shuffling kicking duties, Coach Heisman sent fullback Tommy Spence on the field to kick off.

George Murphy receives the ball on the 5-yard line and takes it to the 15. On the first play of the second half Eddie Edwards runs for a five-yard loss. After three more running plays, Cumberland yields the ball to Tech on the Cumberland 10.

Canty Alexander runs into the nucleus of Cumberland's defense for seven yards, and Strup Strupper closes out the two-play drive with a three-yard scamper into the end zone. Spence makes the point after, and the score is 133–0.

On the ensuing kickoff Spence boots the football through the end zone, a first for the day. This was a feat that very few kickers of this era were able to execute.

Cumberland's offense began the series on the 20 with Murphy being nailed for a 5-yard loss. On second down, Murphy punts, and Buzz Shaver catches the 10-yard kick and returns it 25 yards for a touchdown in the third quarter. After the extra point kick Tech sits on top 140–0.

Spence kicks off again, and Murphy snares the ball at the goal line and runs it for 10 yards. On first down he fumbles, Spence

HIGH SCORING RECORD

Not far into the third quarter of the game Georgia Tech was closing in on the collegiate record for total number points scored. That mark had been set in 1886 when Harvard shellacked Phillips Exeter Academy in New Hampshire.

In this era it was not uncommon for a team to hit the century mark. By 1916 the feat had been accomplished in 186 games. Many of these tilts took place between schools of little recognition. Among the major college teams that have done it are Oklahoma (eight times); Georgia Tech (five times); Yale, Harvard, Michigan, Michigan State, Tennessee and Minnesota (all four times); Princeton, Vanderbilt and Nebraska (three times); Virginia, Georgia, Navy, Notre Dame and Hawaii (two times); and Alabama, Wisconsin, Penn State, Mississippi and Texas A&M (once).

In 1904 Cumberland University beat Bethel 103–0. Georgia Tech's five times to hit triple figures came against Mercer, 105–0, in 1914; Cumberland , 222–0, 1916; N.C. State, 128–0, 1918; the 11th Cavalry, 123–0, 1918; and Furman, 118–0, 1918. All of Tech's 100-plus games came during the Heisman era.

The first two collegiate games to pass the 100 mark were recorded in 1884. Princeton slammed Lafayette 140–0, and Yale crushed Dartmouth 113–0. The most recent game in which the feat took place was in 2003 when Rockford (Illinois) routed Trinity Bible (North Dakota) 105–0.

recovers for Tech at the 10. On the next play Spence finds a gap in the defense and zips into the end zone. After he boots the extra point, the scoreboard reads 147-0.

Instead of receiving the ball, George calls for Cumberland to kick. Eddie Edwards puts his foot into the ball and Tech right end Si Bell returns it 45 yards to the Cumberland 15. On the next play Strupper scores. It's now 154–0.

George dials up Dow Cope's name to receive the next kickoff for the Bulldogs. Cope obliges and returns the kick 10 yards to the Cumberland 35 where the maroon men fumble on the next play.

Following the fumble Heisman appoints Spence to take charge of the next running play for Tech. Spence gallops through the middle of Cumberland's hapless defense and scores. He then kicks the extra point, and at this point history is made with a new record for most points scored in a football game at 161.

Spence kicks again and Murphy returns it to the Cumberland 10. McDonald then loses five yards. Murphy gains three but fumbles at the 8-yard line. Tech recovers and Canty Alexander takes it into the end zone on the first play. Spence misses the extra point, the first errant boot of the day after targeting 23 in a row. Tech's lead blossoms to 167–0.

Murphy takes the next kickoff five yards to the Cumberland 20. In the huddle Cumberland calls two pass plays. Both result in incomplete passes, so McDonald punts. The 35-yard punt is caught by Strupper, who races 55 yards for a touchdown. Spence misses a second extra point attempt, and the score stands at 173–0.

GEORGE THOMAS (GEORGE) MURPHY *graduated from the Cumberland Law School and returned to his hometown of Huntingdon, Tennessee, where he practiced law for a dozen or so years and then moved to Detroit. In Detroit he was named Judge of Recorder's Court, a position he held from 1935 until he retired in 1963. Murphy died in 1983 at the age of 87.*

DOW R. COPE traveled more than 2,300 miles from the northwest tip of the state of Washington to attend Cumberland University. Upon graduation he returned to his home in Yakima, Washington, about 60 miles south of Mt. Rainier. He joined the U.S. Army and was killed during World War I on an airfield near Tours, France. News of his death was published in The Spokane Daily Chronicle on June 22, 1918, 20 months after he participated in the game of his life.

B.F. "BIRD" PATY and C.W. "CHARLIE" WARWICK: Before enrolling into the Cumberland Law School Paty earned an undergraduate degree from the University of North Carolina in 1915. He entered Cumberland in the fall of 1916 and after receiving his law degree returned to his native Tullahoma, Tennessee, where he became a successful attorney. Later he moved to West Palm Beach, Florida to practice law with his teammate Warwick. After earning his law degree from Cumberland, Warwick and his family moved to Florida in 1927 where Paty later joined him, and the two established a successful law practice.

Warwick, an avid golfer, was appointed to the original West Palm Beach Golf Commission by the City of West Palm Beach in 1929. He is credited with saving the golf course and perhaps the West Palm Beach Country Club during World War II when the club was taken over by the U.S. government through the War Powers Act. Warwick in his role as chairman of the City Golf Commission was able to lease the nearby Belvedere golf course in 1942 for $3,000 per month as an interim replacement venue. After the war and following a significant financial settlement with the U.S. government of more than $230,000, the West Palm Beach Country Club was re-established.

Spence kicks off for a final time in the third period. Murphy fields the ball and is tackled immediately for no return. Cumberland begins its series on the 10-yard line where quarterback Murphy throws an errant pass into the arms of Tech's Spence who makes the interception good for six points. Strupper boots the extra point, and the third quarter concludes with the score standing at 180–0.

After the third quarter ends

George rushes to his squad immediately after he hears the whistle blow ending the third quarter. His rag-tag band of brothers has been denigrated by a superior Georgia Tech team.

The group of budding attorneys had been whipped unmercifully. They were despondent and weary.

Not about to leave with still the fourth quarter on tap, Tech's horde of fans were enjoying the slaughter. For the Cumberland players the jeering, mocking and clamor might have been similar to the sounds ineffective gladiators heard in the Rome coliseum two thousand years earlier. Tech supporters were calling for no mercy and demanding more points.

George, while still not harmed physically like his bruised squad although he had substituted himself throughout the afternoon as a backup fullback, was bleeding profusely inside. He knew he was the one responsible for having these friends of his sent to the battlefield.

Washing their faces with wet towels and taking turns guzzling water with a dipper from a wooden bucket, the weary Bulldogs listened to George plea for "just one more 12-minute period."

Meanwhile, Heisman enthusiastically barks new orders to his team. His encouragement is relentless. He continues to hold fast to the same game plan he shared at half time, that his players should be alert and watchful.

"Above all, men, we surely don't want these fellows to slip through our lines, our main defenses, and score on us," he warns.

Coach Heisman knows the more points his team scores the more credit his team will receive as a contender for the 1916 national title. Likewise, he reasons that a score by this pitiful opponent could take his team down a notch in the eyes of sports writers who eventually would be selecting the season's national champion.

Points prove everything

During this era before television and radio game broadcasts and a playoff system, national college football champions were decided for the most part by sports writers who basically gave the highest ranking to the teams scoring the most points.

There were no mercy rules. The more points a team could score against an unworthy opponent the more credit that team would get when rankings were published.

Despite running the score up against Cumberland, John Heisman knew the system was flawed. He often complained to his sports journalist friend Grantland Rice about the injustice of it all.

Heisman showing his disdain for this practice once publicly proffered, "I have often contended that this habit on the part of sports writers of totaling up, from week's end to week's end, the number of points each team has amassed in its various games, and comparing them one with another, was a useless thing, for it means nothing whatever in the way of determining which is the better of an evenly grouped set of college teams. Still the writers persisted and some at each season's end would still presume to hang an argument on what they claimed it showed.

"So, finding that folks are determined to take the crazy thing into consideration, we at Tech determined this year, at the start of the season, to show folks that it is no very difficult thing to run up a score in one easy game, from which it might perhaps be seen that it could be done in other easy games as well."

Be that as it may, Heisman was confident that his team would not be in the running for a national championship if it had taken the pedal off the gas in the Cumberland game and in other games on its schedule. The week before playing Cumberland, Tech defeated Mercer 63–0.

Fourth quarter

There was light, ever so slight, at the end of the tunnel for Cumberland as Tech's Marshall Guill lined up his first kickoff assignment of the afternoon to start the final quarter.

George Murphy handles the kick and is downed by a half dozen Tech players on the 20-yard line. Cumberland's offense huddles and McDonald calls a pass. His throw, more of a lob, is intercepted by Stan Fellers, who returns the ball 40 yards for a touchdown. Bill Fincher boots the extra point, and Tech widens the margin to 187–0.

Guill kicks off again, and again Murphy returns the kick 10 yards to the 30. On first down he tries a run off right tackle for no gain. On second down Eddie Edwards finds a gap in the Tech line for a 5-yard gain to the 35 before he fumbles. Bob Glover recovers for the Engineers. George Griffin then runs wide around right end for 35 yards and scores. Fincher completes the extra point conversion, and Tech's up 194–0.

Guill's kickoff drops into the hands of Cumberland's Eddie Edwards, who returns it 10 yards to the Cumberland 30.

On first down Edwards attempts a run veering to the left. He loses three yards, and Cumberland options to punt on second

HUDDLE INTRODUCED

Several scholars of the game contend that Cumberland was the first team to use the huddle in college football. Some argue the exercise of retreating to a safe distance behind the ball and gathering in a group as Cumberland did several times in its game against Georgia Tech was not so much for planning or scheming about the next play, but rather for Cumberland it was a time to catch a breath and rub a wound.

down. Guill fields McDonald's kick, a 20-yard effort, and returns it 17 yards to the Cumberland 30. From there Glover runs 28 yards on the first play from scrimmage.

Senter takes the next snap and slips through Cumberland's line for a 2-yard skip into the end zone. Fincher makes good the extra point conversion, and the score crosses the 200-point threshold with the score standing at 201–0.

Heisman assigns kickoff duties to Fincher following his extra-point boot. Edwards receives the kick for Cumberland at the goal line and sprints to the 10-yard line before being upended. Murphy then loses three yards on first down, and Edwards loses five yards on the next play. Then McDonald completes a 10-yard pass to Murphy, who is tackled on the 12. It proves to be Cumberland's best offensive gain of the day.

Still far short of a first down marker, Cumberland punts the ball 28 yards to Tech's "fellers". He makes two shifty darts and speeds 40 yards to the end zone. His touchdown with Fincher's extra point tacked on the end raises the score to 208–0.

Tech's Fincher kicks off to Murphy, who returns the ball three yards to the Cumberland 18. Edwards rushes for no gain after which Murphy takes a handoff and fumbles at the line of scrimmage. Senter recovers for Tech advancing the ball three yards before being swarmed by a mob of maroon jerseys. On the next play Fellers rambles 15 yards around left end, finds the end zone, and scores. Fincher kicks the extra point, and Tech's total is 215–0.

Fincher kicks off, and the ball lands in the hands of Warwick who returns the kick five yards to the Bulldog 15. On the next two plays Edwards and McDonald run for no gain. On third down McDonald makes one desperate attempt to complete a pass but he is intercepted by Senter who races 30 yards and scores Georgia Tech's final touchdown of the afternoon. Fincher makes the extra point, and the scoreboard reads at 222–0.

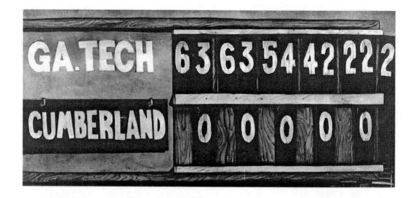

Although the Tech ambush is over, there is time for one last kickoff.

Fincher boots the ball to Gouger, who runs the ball five yards to the 20.

The wrong bench

Nearing the final minutes of the game with a most comfortable lead, Heisman peers down his bench to ensure that all of his players have had a chance to play in the historic game.

Sitting on the end of the pine, he spies a player that doesn't fit. Heisman realizes that the player in the maroon jersey and somewhat deceptively hidden by partially being covered with garb from Tech's athletic department is a Cumberland man.

Approaching the athlete, he inquires, "Aren't you a Cumberland player?"

"Yes sir," the student answers meekly.

"Son, you need to get back on the other side of the field," Heisman says, believing the young law student might have taken a blow to the head on the previous play, leaving him dazed.

However the student looks back at the coach, shakes his head from side to side and explains, "No, sir, Mr. Heisman, this is the right bench. If I go over there, they'll put me back in the game!"

Seeing the humor in the situation, Coach Heisman smiles, orders a blanket for the Cumberland student, tells him to cover up, and gives him permission to remain on the Tech bench until the game expires.

Back on the field Cumberland is huddling for the grand finale. The teammates decide that Eddie Edwards should be given the honor of carrying the ball. He takes the snap and is downed for a 5-yard loss.

The whistle blows, and the massacre comes to a halt. The game is officially over.

CHAPTER
TWELVE

PRESS ALLOWS NO MERCY

No first downs

In *The Atlanta Constitution* on the day of the game a headline was published at the top of page ten that screamed in bold caps **YELLOW JACKETS PLAY CUMBERLAND**. A subhead added "Local Eleven Should Have Easy Sailing In Today's Game — Game Starts at 3 O'clock."

For a contest that notched 32 touchdowns, analysts have noted that it is ironic that there were no first downs recorded by either team. Cumberland never logged a first down because its offense couldn't move the ball forward 10 yards in a single series. Tech didn't have a first down because its offense scored a touchdown within four plays on every possession.

The Engineers never threw a pass, never punted and never fumbled.

Tech's offense gained a total of 978 yards on 28 plays. Tech's defense claimed another 642 yards while advancing Cumberland turnovers.

Tech scored 10 touchdowns on first-down plays and 14 touchdowns on interceptions, fumbles or kick returns. Tech rambled for 220 yards on punt returns, scoring five touchdowns and matched another 220 yards on kickoff returns scoring one touchdown.

Tech's only miscues for the afternoon came on two misguided extra-point attempts, but their kickers hit a record 30 of 32 extra-points tries.

Pitiful Cumberland went backwards with a minus 42 yards rushing but did garner 14 yards in the right direction on two pass completions. Of their 16 other passes, six were intercepted and ten were knocked away or dropped. Cumberland yielded the ball nine times due to fumbles.

Cumberland's longest play of the day was a 10-yard pass, but that play came on a fourth down and 22, thus it did not result in a first down.

The NCAA, founded in 1937, doesn't list records set in the Cumberland vs. Georgia Tech game, but several happenings in the game have yet to be matched in any other collegiate football game since.

Numerous records were set in the game, many of which still stand including most points scored in a collegiate football game, most touchdowns in a game (32), most points scored in a quarter (63 in the first quarter), most individual players to score a touchdown in a single game (13), most touchdowns in a quarter (9), most points scored in a half (126), most extra points kicked in a game (30), and most extra points kicked in a game by one player (18 by Jim Preas). Other Tech kickers for the day were Tommy Spence, Thomasville, Ga.; Marshall Guill, Sparta, Ga.; and Bill Fincher, Spring Place, Ga.

After the game

Heisman traditionally treated his team to a steak dinner when he believed they had played a game worthy of such a reward. This had been such a game.

But before steaks were served, he put his players through a thorough workout.

After final goodbyes were being said and handshakes exchanged, Heisman blew a long brisk note on his whistle and ordered his team back to the field.

This was not unexpected. His team had seen the drill before. Over the next half hour they went back into combat but this time against each other. Heisman felt his squad had not had a sufficient physical experience for the day.

Satisfied with their efforts, he called his team together at the center of the field. He told the players, "You men played a pretty good game out there today. What do you say we eat some beefsteak?"

The Georgia Tech boys responded with hurrahs.

Cumberland's bunch by now had limped and staggered their way to the bus that transported them to their hotel.

The only positive emotion they felt was that of relief. They had done what they had come to Atlanta to do. Their mission fulfilled in their own way, they too had been successful. The sports world may have looked down on them as losers. But they completed the task that had been placed before them, thus, in their own crumpled condition, they sort of felt they, too, were winners.

Before George and his Bulldogs boarded their bus, Heisman himself presented the student manager a check for $500, the amount Georgia Tech had agreed to pay Cumberland to play the game. As he did so, he extended his hand as if to say all is forgotten, but, with a smirk peeling across his left cheek, the wily Heisman suggested "maybe we can get together again next spring for a baseball game?"

George felt a slight sting at the departing words. Without a doubt, Heisman had gotten his revenge and then some.

Sports writers have a field day

The fact that Cumberland University did not actually have a competitive football team in 1916 had been lost to most sports writers when the national press filed its reports about Georgia Tech's ambush on the tiny Lebanon school.

Few words were written in defense of Cumberland playing the game to fulfill a contract even though the private school's leadership had voted to disband the football program eight months earlier.

Absent also was the fact that the Cumberland team was comprised mainly of law school students and a sprinkling of liberal arts majors who volunteered to play the game with no college football experience.

There was no mention of Heisman insisting that the game be played or he would see to it that Cumberland would pay $3,000 for breach of contract, which could have closed the educational institution.

Writing for *The Atlanta Journal*, Morgan Blake described
the Cumberland team as "pitifully weak opposition" for the
Engineers.

"With all due regard to the Tech team, it must be admitted
that the tremendous score was due more to the pitifully weak
opposition than to any unnatural strength on the part of the
victors. In fact, as a general rule, the only thing necessary for a
touchdown was to give a Tech back the ball and holler, 'Here he
comes' and 'There he goes.'

"The Lebanon boys were absolutely minus any apparent
football virtues. They couldn't run the ball, they couldn't block,
and they couldn't tackle. At spasmodic intervals they were able to
down a runner, but they were decidedly too light and green to be
effective at any stage of the game," Blake wrote.

The report in *The New York Times* was much the same on the day
following the game. The Times story referred to Tech's aggressive
offense and how it had overrun Cumberland's defense.

"When the game began, Georgia Tech scored on its first play.
Cumberland fumbled on the next play, and Tech returned it for
a touchdown. Cumberland fumbled again on its first play, and
Tech returned it for a touchdown. Cumberland fumbled again on
its first play, and Tech scored two plays later. And on and on," *The
Times* report noted.

Similar accounts of the game were filed in Chicago, Boston
and other major cities. It was important to Heisman that the
media had picked up on the game and was reporting the
outcome, especially in the northeast where American football had
been conceived, a region where the schools remained darlings of
a prejudiced press.

Heisman's objective for playing Cumberland had been met.
Beyond payback this lopsided high-scoring affair alerted the
national press corps that his Georgia Tech Engineers might be
something special.

Basking in the spotlight, he was delighted to find himself being anointed as the next best mind in college football, and his Georgia Tech team was moving closer to its coveted goal of becoming a national champion.

CHAPTER
THIRTEEN

LOSERS
AWAY,
HEROES
AT HOME

Back to Lebanon

Early Sunday morning the Cumberland players and their entourage boarded a train bound for Birmingham.

The players and their followers were rather subdued after a night of celebration in Atlanta that had lasted well into the early morning hours.

Emotions were mixed. Their cause for celebration was complicated. There really was no reason to rejoice, but they had completed their mission and, miraculously, no one had been seriously injured.

As the train neared Birmingham the conductor told passengers they would be allowed to get off and mosey about the terminal and stretch their legs or grab a bite to eat.

Terminal Station in Birmingham was as magnificent as Atlanta's train station by the same name. Built in 1909, this station was a main stop for trains representing six railroad companies.

The conductor reported to the travelers that the train would be at rest for an hour and fifteen minutes before departing for Nashville.

With less than a full hour to spend in the station, the Cumberland bunch filed off as quickly as they could. They shuffled to the end of the platform and made a right turn before walking another fifty yards to the station.

Passengers exiting other trains had the same idea. Everywhere the Cumberland group turned there was a lengthy line of waiting customers.

George suggested that they spread out. Everyone, he insisted, doesn't need to go to the same concession area, restaurant, or restroom. The players heeded his advice and divided into groups of two or three and went to fulfill their needs.

Shoeshine stand news

George stays in the first line he joined with the notion of purchasing a ham and cheese sandwich and a Coca-Cola.

Glancing around, he spots a boutique shoeshine stand and a news rack where an elderly African-American man conducts the business of putting a spit shine on the leather cap toe dress shoes of mostly white male passengers flitting about through the station.

Engulfed on three sides of his booth by a massive collection of Sunday newspapers, the shoeshine specialist augments his daily livelihood by peddling the news of the day. Earlier this morning trains from Atlanta, Louisville, New Orleans, Memphis, Nashville, Cincinnati, St. Louis and Chicago have trucked in papers from across their respective departing regions.

George decides to forgo breakfast and makes a bee line to a shoeshine booth.

COST OF GOODS IN 1916

A loaf of bread cost about a nickel as did a bottle of Coke and a ticket to the movie theater (popular at the time was a news reel about the 1912 sinking of the Titanic). Gas was 16 cents a gallon (equivalent to a 2015 price of about $3.15 cents), coffee was about 30 cents a pound, and several leading hotels advertised room rates at $2 per night with meals served at 50 cents each. Car prices began as low as $400. Chevrolet listed its new Chevy 490 at $490, which just happened to be the same price of its greatest competitor, the Model T Ford. Soon after Chevy made the announcement introducing its 490 model, Henry Ford dropped the price of his Model T to $440.

His eye catches a number of headlines in the various newspapers. Several had made mention of the game played the day before in Atlanta, but only as teasers in an effort to lure readers inside to an area reserved for sports fanatics.

The Birmingham News, The Louisville Courier-Journal, Atlanta Constitution, among others, reported the devastating loss Cumberland had suffered at the hands of Georgia Tech.

Details of the game varied in each newspaper. Some of the publications misspelled names. Others omitted names, mainly the names of Cumberland players, but each paper did report the score correctly.

Reading the results, "Georgia Tech 222, Cumberland 0" in newsprint for the first time left George feeling a bit desperate. He had no clue the match would generate so much interest from the press.

Reports about the game and what it meant for Georgia Tech's drive for a national championship had been published in daily newspapers across the nation. What George believed to be not such a big deal turned out to be humongous.

Even the old man shining shoes, born 20 years before the start of the Civil War, who could barely read, could determine from the bold-faced size type on the sports page in The Constitution that Cumberland, as he might put it, had gotten "an old-fashioned whupping" in Atlanta.

Hearing the elderly black man's perspective on the game, George decided to climb up into the customer's chair, where he could rest his feet while his shoes were being shined.

He really had no need of a shine but wanted to hear more about what the old fellow thought about the game.

George listened intently as the shoeshine man told him the reactions he had heard from others, even from a few who had attended the game.

The old man told George that his life had not yet provided him the opportunity of seeing a football game, but it was something he would like to witness one day. He confessed to his customer that the sport didn't make that much sense to him.

He struggled with the idea of congregations of grown men pounding and smashing into one another just to move a funny-shaped ball down a cow pasture. He said that from what he'd heard, the game was more like a back-alley brawl.

George paid attention to every word but really he wanted to know what other people may have been saying about the Cumberland athletes.

George pressed gently for more gossip.

The old man told him that from what he had gathered this Coach Heisman was something else. He relayed to George that folks who had sat in this same chair earlier in the day were saying the Tech team that had beaten the little school from Tennessee would likely win the championship this year. He said they kept saying they'd never seen a football game in which so many points had been scored. They talked about how Heisman was the best coach in the country.

George paid two bits for the old man's artisan work and flipped him a silver dollar as a tip. He walked away with his shoes sporting a handsome shine and felt a bit better hearing that most of the scuttlebutt surrounding the game was about the strength of Tech and not the incompetence of Cumberland.

The student manager had known his team was bad, but he never wanted them to be thought of as cowards or as a group that had disgraced their alma mater.

He was fearful of what the word would be around Lebanon after they returned to the campus.

He hoped the team would receive some sort of a small homecoming after they reached the Lebanon depot and that they might get at least a little praise and considerable credit for helping the college keep its word and perhaps more importantly keeping its doors open.

With low spirits George rounded up his players and the traveling party to make sure all got back to the train on time.

They boarded and departed Birmingham for Nashville, the next and final station before Lebanon.

Back in Lebanon

After a thirty-minute stop in Nashville the train rolled east toward Lebanon. The train was scheduled to arrive at 3:42 p.m.

From Nashville the train picked up passengers at three stops that included Hermitage, a neighborhood community near the home of the late President Andrew Jackson; Mt. Juliet, a farm community on the west side of Wilson County, about 12 miles from Lebanon; and finally before arriving at the final destination, Horn Springs, the place where much of the hoopla for the trip to Atlanta was inspired.

As the train got closer to home, the boys on the team began stirring from their seats. They weren't exactly proud of their efforts, but, by damn, they had given it all they had. Beat-up, worn-out and exhausted, they were content that they had accomplished their mission.

The iron horse's engineer gave two blasts on the horn as it crossed South Cumberland Street only two blocks from the Lebanon station.

As the Cumberland group gazes out windows they see what appears to be a large welcoming crowd awaiting them from the station platform.

Those on board began to hear a band and cheering and then they spied a crowd of two hundred to three hundred people flanking the train. The hoard, which included President Hill, professors, students and town people, were there to greet the heroes who had saved Cumberland University.

Off the train the players scattered. They kissed girlfriends, shook hands with comrades and even hugged strangers as they made the most of their emotional return.

Back in Atlanta

Coach Heisman had accomplished his goals on Saturday. He had thoroughly embarrassed Cumberland. He had gotten the payback he had so desperately sought since his baseball team had suffered the humiliating defeat at the hands of Cumberland and George Allen the previous spring. And he had captured the attention of sports writers across the nation with the enormous number of points his team had scored.

The following Sunday afternoon he was back in his office on the Tech campus studying his next opponent.

Tech would be playing Davidson on October 14. The North Carolina college had lost its first game of the season 14–0 to Virginia but beat North Carolina State 16–0 in its second outing.

Davidson would be a formidable opponent. Heisman's task was to prepare his team for a real team after the easy trouncing of Cumberland.

Georgia Tech was clearly on a route that could take them to a national championship, the first for the Engineers and the first for their already highly decorated coach.

None other than Grantland Rice was proclaiming Heisman as the next great mind and coach in college football. Attracting the attention of a myriad of sports writers was the fact that Tech had scored 285 points in its first two games and not allowed its opponents to score. No other team in the nation had ever come close to such a feat.

The stars were aligning, and Heisman was cognizant of the opportunity before him.

His single most concern was to keep his team focused. They had seven more games on their schedule. One slip up, one fumble, one interception, one dropped punt, one missed tackle could cost them a game. And one lost game could be the difference between winning a national championship and having to wait till next year.

Again and again Coach Heisman reminded his players about the disciplines that create winners.

Developing a strategy for the game against Davidson, he would be well prepared for the team presentation he would deliver at practice on Monday afternoon.

On the Cumberland campus

While the jubilant welcome at the train depot had proved exhilarating to the valiant losers, Cumberland University President Hill did not believe the celebration on Sunday was all that it should have been.

The results of the game had reached campus late Saturday via Western Union, although there still were many who had not gotten the word. There were also a great number of people from town, outside the Cumberland family, who had made financial contributions for the cause, and they too, Hill reckoned, should have the opportunity to congratulate the team and join the celebration.

On Monday afternoon Hill summonsed to his office in Memorial Hall key members of his administrative team, a small delegation of trustees, George Allen, and several members of the law school faculty to discuss how to plan an event worthy of the expedition to Atlanta.

As the group sat in Hill's office waiting for the meeting to begin, conspicuously absent was George, the primary principal for whom the meeting had been called.

A few minutes past 3 p.m. Hill, assured that all were present, explained that he had intentionally asked George to arrive around 3:15 p.m. Starting from day one of the entire ordeal, Hill revisited for those in his office the sacrifice that had been made, George's commitment to right a grievous personal mistake, and what this had meant for the sustainability of Cumberland University.

As he wound down his summary of the story, he told those present that in a few minutes George would be entering the room, and he asked that each of them stand and offer a rousing ovation for the young man whom he described as possibly Cumberland's most outstanding law student.

A slight rap came on the door, and George walked into the room where he was met by a vigorous standing ovation, a dozen hearty slaps on the back and three choruses of "For He's a Jolly Good Fellow."

The Mississippi native was overwhelmed. George tried to begin to speak, his voice trembling, as he stood astonished in front of this august audience.

Among those greeting George were Judge Nathan Green Jr., 89, the first dean of the Cumberland University School of Law (Judge Green taught at the law school until his death at age 92); Professor of Law Andrew Bennett Martin, an 1858 graduate of Cumberland and former major and adjutant on the staffs of Confederate Generals Robert Hatton, George Dibreil, and Joseph Wheeler; Professor of Moot Court Proceedings Edward Ewing Beard, a former Lebanon mayor and member of the state legislature; Professor W.P. Graham, who along with Hill was in charge of the university's athletic programs; and three members of the university's board of trust including Amzl W. Hooker, James Lee Weir, and Selden R. Williams.

Represented in the president's office with George was a select portfolio of individuals who had personally overseen triumphs and defeats throughout much of Cumberland's history. A few had seen Cumberland rise from the ashes after its main building was torched and burned to the ground by Union troops at the end of the Civil War. A couple of these men were instrumental in turning the university's law school into one of the nation's finest, and several of the trustees, successful local businessmen, had stood by Cumberland through periods of severe financial woes.

George tried his best to exercise control over his emotions as he spoke briefly. He related the challenges in simply getting the team to and back from Atlanta. He named each player and offered a brief profile of every man. He apologized for being the one responsible for causing the game to be played in the first place. And he gave a terse description of what had taken place on the gridiron. Those to whom he was speaking had little knowledge about the sport.

President Hill broke in at an appropriate moment to steer the discussion back on track as they needed to plan a party to recognize George and his band of football players.

They decided a Friday afternoon parade along Main Street and around the square would be just the ticket with a barbecue picnic Saturday afternoon on the campus green. Both events were to be publicized in the Cumberland Weekly, the student publication, and in The Lebanon Banner, the local newspaper published each Thursday.

Hill closed with a declaration that George had helped turn back the pages of time when a former Cumberland alumnus wrote a single word, "Resurgam," on a fragment of a burned and frail column that once supported the university's first administrative building, a casualty of the fire in the remaining days of the Civil War.

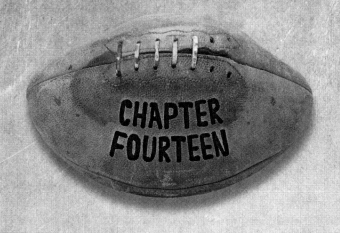

FOOTBALL IN THE SOUTH BOOMS

Sports coverage had limitations

Sports writers from coast to coast continued to write reams of copy filling hot-type galleys days after Tech had demolished Cumberland.

The game may have been yesterday's news, but John Heisman and his undefeated Georgia Tech team, only two weeks into the season, were the talk of the nation.

Covering sports in the early decades of the 20th century was largely a chore left to a few columnists mostly in the Northeast. Writers such as Grantland Rice were relegated to let other sports journalists know what they had learned or observed. They were the eyes and ears for much of the nation.

What they saw and what they determined to be the advantage of one team over another, the superior talent of a single player, the speed of a running back, or the tenacity of a coach would appear in print a couple of days after a game. This same cadre of writers greatly influenced others when it came time to select All-American teams and name national champions.

There were obvious restraints with respect to travel making it difficult to go from one venue to another several hundred miles apart because there were few commercial flights and rail passage could take days depending on connecting schedules. Communication technology was limited to telephone and tele-graph. There were few options available for writers who might be on the West Coast attempting to publish a story about a team or sporting event in Georgia, Alabama, and Tennessee or on the East Coast.

It was therefore necessary for many to rely on the descriptive accounts of a few. While scores and only briefs may be reported the day following a game in newspapers a significant distance away from where a game had been played, the complete, more detailed coverage of a game might not appear until days later, when a writer would recreate play-by-play details from a story posted in a major market by Grantland Rice and his peers and received in his newsroom by U.S. Mail.

Several newspapers published reports about the Cumberland vs. Georgia Tech game. But many did not show up in print until a week or so later after the game, particularly newspapers outside of the Southeast.

For example the *Taylor Daily Press* in Taylor, Texas, didn't publish its story about the game until October 16, nine days after the game. Even at this late date the newspaper's sports department believed the story merited a two-column, two-line headline, "What a Grid Game, Georgia Wins 222–0," and 25 column inches of news hole space. Although the newspaper gave a full account of the story accurately, its headline misidentified the name of the winning school.

Football, although growing in popularity, was not yet enjoyed nationwide. The sport had originated in the Northeast and it was there where it was still the most popular. If there was a headquarters during this era, it would have been in the heart of the Ivy League. Harvard, Yale, Dartmouth, Pennsylvania and others in the Northeast were the dominant forces in the sport.

All measurements and comparisons to teams in other parts of the country were based on what successes and accomplishments had been recorded by the best playing the game in the Ivy League.

Because of the newness of the sport in much of the country, sports writers tended to describe games in colorful verbiage including an abundance of adverbs and first-person pronouns.

An excellent example of this style of journalism can be found in a report of the Cumberland vs. Georgia Tech game published in the Oct. 17, 1916, edition of *The Washington Times*. *The Times* scribe wrote, "The performance of Georgia Tech against Cumberland at Atlanta Saturday, October 7, invites our attention to the subject of huge scores. In this game Tech, affectionately known throughout the South as the Yellow Jackets, submerged Cumberland under the unprecedented score of 222 points to 0."

Record score unlocks gates for the South

Tech's scoring assault on Cumberland accomplished three achievements besides the record score itself.

First, it served to unlock the well-guarded gates that had kept football programs in the South hidden from the same recognition bestowed by the national press on teams in the Northeast. Perhaps for the first time since the beginning of the game, sports writers across the U.S., seeing the number of points scored by Tech, were realizing that teams in the South can also be credible.

Secondly, the record point total made it almost a newsroom requirement that a report of the game be published in newspapers stretching from Texas to Philadelphia. If Tech had not scored the 222 points it did, its game against Cumberland may not have been newsworthy, and certainly not of the caliber to merit the nation-wide coverage it received.

For Georgia Tech the third consequence of the final score was possibly the most important.

While the game caused sports writers to look to the South for outstanding football teams, they looked first at Georgia Tech. No other school in the nation had scored so many points in one game.

Writers covering a college sports beat in Texas, Boston, Chicago, or Washington had to be impressed with the 222 points posted on the scoreboard. They might not have known anything about Cumberland, but they were ready to believe that any team that could rack up this high a score must surely be one of the strongest teams in the country.

Although the score drew much attention to the game, the relationship John Heisman shared with Grantland Rice didn't hurt. Rice, now at or near the pinnacle of his career, was considered the dean of sports writers. For many in the fourth estate he was credited with having the greatest influence leading to a movement in journalism that provided for a respectful place for sports writers in the newsroom.

Until Rice's appearance in Nashville, Atlanta, and New York, and the great following of readers he attracted through sports columns published nationwide, sports writing and the "sporting news," as it was labeled in past years, was largely regarded as a secondary class of journalism.

Hundreds of thousands read Rice's columns during the era. His readers were turning into football enthusiasts. His columns, syndicated in the *New York Tribune*, were reprinted in newspapers, big and small, across the nation.

America was learning that other schools outside the Northeast were playing a quality brand of the game, and one of those universities was Georgia Tech.

Tech's victory over Cumberland was a wake-up call that rang with a loud alarm that football was alive and thriving in the South. The clarion call, heard clearest in the Northeast, signaled that other southern schools soon would be getting their due from national sports writers, and no longer would colleges in one neck of the woods get preferential treatment when it came to picking a national champion.

It was a new day for football in the South, with the door opened by Heisman and his Georgia Tech Yellow Jackets.

News about Georgia Tech's football team swept the nation. The Engineers were getting accolades from football fans in 48 states.

There have been few college teams with as many nicknames accepted by Georgia Tech.

The school's early teams were called Engineers. From 1893 to 1910 the football team was simply called the "Techs." In 1902 some Southern newspapers began calling the university's teams the Blacksmiths because of the large amount of metal work that was being completed in the Institute's Mechanical and Manufacturing departments.

Beginning in 1905, *The Atlanta Constitution* referred to the Tech squad as the Yellowjackets (one word) because of the yellow jackets that team supporters often wore to their games.

The monikers Engineers and Yellow Jackets have been staples ever since, while in some circles they have become known as the Rambling Wreck.

In 1917 sports writers proclaimed Georgia Tech as the Golden Tornadoes because of the domineering style of play exhibited by Heisman's team on offense.

Continuing to display his genius, the coach's offense attracted much attention early in the 1916 season with the introduction of backfield shifts, the quarterback standing over center and taking a direct snap, a single-wing formation, and the premiere of a series of plays from what would become known as the "T" formation.

Following a 32–10 win against Davidson in 1917, Hal Reynolds, writing for *The Atlanta Constitution*, wrote, "While no credit must be taken from Davidson for the game fight they put up in the face of big odds, it was evident the Golden Tornado, as the Tech team has been dubbed, was not the whirlwind it was one week before against Pennsylvania."

That was the first time the term Golden Tornado was applied to Tech's football squad.

Game three: Tech vs. Davidson

A week had passed since the blowout against Cumberland. For Coach Heisman's squad it was a matter of getting back to business.

The routine was the same as it was a week ago and the week before that. Even so, Heisman, the consummate glass is half-empty personality, was expressing to his players his worries about Davidson.

He urged his players, untested by the season's first two outings, to be aware of their surroundings, to be disciplined

RAMBLIN' WRECK FROM GEORGIA TECH

Georgia Tech's rallying theme song had its beginning, according to alumnus Howard Cutter, a member of the university's first graduating class in 1892, during the first two years when the school opened in 1885. The earliest published version of the song is believed to have appeared in 1908 in the *Blueprint*, the Georgia Tech yearbook. The song has been sung on various occasions from athletic events to alumni gatherings and even sung during a 1959 meeting in Moscow between Vice President Richard Nixon and Russia Premier Nikita Khrushchev.

RAMBLIN' WRECK

I'm a Ramblin' Wreck from Georgia Tech and a hell of an engineer,
A helluva, helluva, helluva, helluva, hell of an engineer,
Like all the jolly good fellows, I drink my whiskey clear,
I'm a Ramblin' Wreck from Georgia Tech and a hell of an engineer.
Oh, if I had a daughter, sir, I'd dress her in White and Gold,
And put her on the campus, to cheer the brave and bold.
But if I had a son, sir, I'll tell you what he'd do.
He would yell, "To Hell with Georgia," like his daddy used to do.
Oh, I wish I had a barrel of rum and sugar three thousand pounds,
A college bell to put it in and a clapper to stir it around.
I'd drink to all good fellows who come from far and near.
I'm a rambling,' gamblin,' hell of an engineer.

in their play, and to think and use their heads. Heisman always preached to players to not make stupid, thoughtless mistakes.

He'd given the same lecture to the same 38 players seven days ago. And the words he spoke then echoed the pre-game message he had delivered two weeks earlier when Tech opened its season by annihilating Mercer 63–0.

Heisman's challenge now was sober up his team from the elixir of victory, two games in which they walloped their opponents by a collective score of 285–0.

He had to get his team focused for Davidson, a team that had the mettle to upend his Engineers, although the Wildcats' play had not been dominating.

Davidson lost its first game to a not-so-ferocious Virginia team 14–0. However, they won the second game on their schedule.

While Tech was trouncing Cumberland, Davidson was handing North Carolina State its first loss for the year, a 16–0 decision.

Heisman, evaluating Davidson, saw a team that would be passionately energized to beat a school that had walked over its first two opponents.

Played at home in Atlanta, the game progressed much as Heisman had feared. His offense was playing with what appeared to be as one sports writer noted "little effort." The team was sluggish.

At half time Heisman delivered a crystal clear message. He advised his players that if they did not begin playing to their capabilities, they would get socked by a much weaker Davidson team, and they would be out of the running for the national championship.

Message received

The Engineers rallied in the second half, won the game scoring nine points and held the opposition scoreless.

Heisman was disturbed because he realized that the team
from whom Tech had narrowly escaped was not that tough, and
as it turned out Davidson struggled to eke out a winning season
finishing with a 5–3–1 record.

Georgia Tech's squeak-by win garnered as much nationwide
coverage as its 222–0 rout over Cumberland the week before.
The stories being published this time were slanted more towards
"what happened?"

That same Saturday

A week had passed since George Allen had taken his fraternity
boys to Atlanta.

As he and his brothers gathered with hundreds for a campus
and community celebration, they couldn't help but think about
the stage they were on seven days ago. Now they were back in
Lebanon in their safe environment and all was well.

The town in cooperation with the Cumberland administration
was hosting a parade along West Main Street in honor of the team
of still bruised and battered volunteers, followed by a barbecue
picnic of sorts on the campus. There were lots of speeches and lots
of praise heaped upon George and his disciples for their efforts in
saving their school.

A canopy of golden and ruby leaves hovered over the front
lawn of Memorial Hall. The crowd wrapped themselves in
sweaters as they sipped ice tea and lemonade and devoured pork
ribs, barbecue, and chicken that had been slow smoked over open
pits since the early morning hours.

It was a very good day for Cumberland University.

No one at the affair was concerned about the press coverage
that would follow. Cumberland, after its one and only official
game of an unofficial season, had provided all the material necessary for the sports writers to practice their prose. And now that
had passed.

It was time to soak in the splendor and then get back to the business at hand, more moot court proceedings, research on court decisions, contracts and tort law, and how to defend an innocent man charged with murder.

Not quite back to the books

The loss, although anticipated, was still devastating for the Cumberland squad, even days after the battle. Some members of the maroon team had played football in high school and others had starred in sandlot pick-up games.

The rag-tag athletic experience had created even stronger ties of friendship while their admiration for their student leader had also risen as had their sentiments for their alma mater.

And they were not quite ready to hang up their cleats.

What was to be a one and done campaign for Cumberland in 1916 actually resulted in a schedule according to several newspaper reports with four additional games.

One of these contests, likely a warmup before the trip to Atlanta, was a whopping 107–0 loss to Sewanee on September 30, only days before the Tech game.

After the Tech game there are unsubstantiated reports of the Bulldogs taking on non-collegiate teams in Bowling Green, Ky., Hartsville, Tenn., and Nashville.

Reviews peeve Heisman

Coach Heisman was not pleased with his team's performance against a minimal opponent like Davidson and not at all pleased with the copy appearing in the national press.

His 1916 campaign had stalled.

Next up for the Engineers was North Carolina.

The engagement would be an interesting test for the undefeated Tech team, and a strong showing could put them back near the front of the pack.

North Carolina won its first game, defeating Wake Forrest 20–0. After that they ventured north of the Mason-Dixon Line and tackled two Ivy League schools, Princeton and Harvard.

Princeton topped the boys from the south 29–0, and Harvard smacked them 20–0.

Georgia Tech needed badly to whip North Carolina in a fashion akin to its wins over Mercer and Cumberland.

Heisman sharpened his message to his Engineers and continued to accent his essentials of winning football and prayed for an outcome that would speak to the strength of his team and the caliber of football being played by universities in the South.

Georgia Tech did beat North Carolina but not in the convincing style that Heisman had hoped. The Yellow Jackets won 10–6, but the team that had been unable to score against its previous Ivy League opponents managed to score six points against Tech and held Heisman's offense to a mere touchdown and field goal.

Although still undefeated, Georgia Tech's reputation as a gridiron powerhouse had slipped another notch.

The national press continued to heap praise on teams in the North and Northeast, while they discounted those in the boll weevil states of the South.

Other campaigns

While Georgia Tech, Harvard, Pittsburgh, and other college powers were campaigning for a national football championship, there was bigger news on the front page about events at home and abroad.

War raged in Europe, a revolution was taking place in Mexico, and much of the U.S. was focused on a presidential election set for the first Tuesday in November.

Woodrow Wilson, the incumbent Democrat, was campaigning to keep the White House, while his Republican opponent, U.S.

Supreme Court Justice Charles Evans Hughes, was campaigning to have voters boot him out of office.

Cumberland University had a role in the election in that Hughes had been a colleague of Cumberland graduate Justice Horace Harmon Lurton, who served with him on the U.S. Supreme Court. While campaigning in Tennessee and Kentucky, Hughes capitalized on their relationship as a point of reference in many of his stump speeches and introductions. Despite his attempts to attract voters in Tennessee and Kentucky by sharing anecdotes about his time on the bench with Lurton, both states went for Wilson.

Wilson won the election with a 600,000 popular vote margin; however, the vote in the Electoral College was much closer. He edged Hughes by only 23 votes, 277–254.

The incumbent's win was not necessarily a good omen for football in the South and certainly not for Georgia Tech.

Wilson, a football fan who had coached at Wesleyan University, had also served as president of Princeton. His loyalty to the Ivy League remained solid, and that could pose another problem for John Heisman as he tried to crack the mindset that college football supremacy prevailed in the Northeast.

Week five

Tech would pass the halfway point of their nine-game season with the contest against Washington and Lee at Grant Field on October 28.

Washington and Lee also had posted a record of 2–1–1. Although not a particularly strong team, they had garnered some national attention from their battles against Army and Rutgers.

A very good Army team beat them 14–7, and they tied Rutgers 13–13 in New Jersey.

There were a couple of interesting considerations surrounding the Tech game with Washington and Lee.

It would be a game watched closely by sports writers across the nation since Washington and Lee had played its previous two games in the Northeast with mixed results.

And frankly the jury was still out on Heisman's Georgia Tech team.

The decision would be made for the good if Heisman could blow out Washington and Lee as he had Mercer and Cumberland. But a Tech loss, tie or a win by a small margin would leave them in the dust.

To really kick the team into high gear, Heisman had searchlights brought into Grant Field so that his team could practice at night. He practiced his boys hard and lectured them even more sternly.

It was to no avail as Tech managed a 7–7 tie with Washington and Lee. If they had been a listing on the stock market, they would have dropped 50 points.

At the bottom of *The Washington Herald* sports page on Sunday morning, the all-caps headline blared, "WASHINGTON AND LEE PLAYS TECH A TIE." The capsule-like summary of the game covered only two column inches of type.

Tech's collapse sets stage for 1917

Four games remained on the Engineers' schedule, but for all practical purposes their shot at the national championship was gone.

Heisman pressed forward, inspiring his team to finish the season with their best efforts, hoping that they might receive some honorable mentions and if nothing else lay the groundwork for 1917. He reckoned that if his squad could end the schedule with blue-chip wins, he could get a head start on next year.

Georgia Tech's final four games were with Tulane, Alabama, Georgia and Auburn. The quartet had fielded highly respected teams for the season and each ended the season with winning records.

The Engineers responded to their mentor's call for picking up the pieces by crushing Tulane, scoring 45 points and holding their opponent scoreless.

The next week Georgia Tech topped Alabama 13–0.

And the week following the Engineers collared the Georgia Bulldogs 21–0.

Tech's final game was against a touted Auburn squad.

Auburn came to Grant Field with six wins and a single loss.

The Tigers had been upended by Vanderbilt the week before the Tech game, but had whipped Samford, Mercer, Clemson, Mississippi State, Georgia and Florida.

Heisman cautioned his boys that Auburn would not be easy. He believed they would be hungry after losing their first game of the year.

Heisman had coached on the plains at Auburn from 1895–1899. He was 30 years young when he left his Auburn for Clemson but old enough to know the school nurtured a winning spirit.

Georgia Tech answered his challenge and responded by clipping the War Eagles 33–7.

In the end the sports writers were generous. Columnists wrote that it was a good season for Georgia Tech and its brainy coach, the man of innovation.

Heisman was not elated, but he was satisfied that Tech had made a name for itself on college football's national stage.

CHAPTER
FIFTEEN

WINNING
IT ALL

Next year is here

Disappointed but not discouraged, Coach Heisman began planning in the early summer for the 1917 version of the Golden Tornadoes.

Several Tech players and almost all the fans that had crowded Grant Field in 1916 had adopted the battle cry of "Wait 'til Next Year." Heisman didn't like it, but nonetheless he had little control over what the fans did or did not do and over what might be going through the minds of his players. As a strict disciplinarian, he could dictate what his players said aloud but not even John Heisman could manage or audit their thoughts.

Confidentially, he believed his 1917 team, at least on paper, looked terrific. One of the main factors leading him to that opinion was running back Strup Strupper.

No defensive line could contain the lively lad who ran at will on Saturday afternoons. Strupper would be back a bit faster and a lot stronger. The senior was easily one of the finest running backs in the country.

FIRST ALL-AMERICAS FROM DEEP SOUTH

Everett (Strup) Strupper was selected a consensus All-America in 1917 and also picked was teammate Walker Glenn (Bill) "Big Six" Carpenter. Their selection to the All-America team represented the first two players from the Deep South to receive the honor. Strupper, from Columbus, Ga., was a Tech mainstay in the offensive backfield for three years. Carpenter, a mechanical engineering major from Newnan, Georgia, played tackle and end.

Complimenting Strup's talent would be an offensive line packed with returning lettermen. These eleven were going to be explosive off the ball and would make good on their recently anointed nickname the Golden Tornadoes.

Things to do

College football head coaches during the early 1900s had added responsibilities that went far beyond designing offensive strategies and plotting defensive blockades. There were no administrative staffs, no athletic directors, no equipment managers and no outside financial help such as a booster club. The coach served as sole proprietor and caretaker of the team.

Smaller schools like Cumberland would rely on student managers to arrange games and keep the locker room organized, while the coach was left with player personnel matters and the pure necessities of coaching.

Looking forward to the fall, Heisman had a lengthy to-do list before he welcomed his team back to Atlanta.

High on that list was the need to check, re-check and confirm the teams on the schedule. In order to have a championship season, Tech would need to win all nine games. A forfeit by an opponent would be a liability, and that was certainly a possibility with some colleges dropping the sport as the United States entered the war in Europe in April. Thus, the rosters of many college teams had been stripped of some of their athletes.

Responding to the matter, the Walter Camp Football Foundation decided that it would not name a 1917 All-America team. Instead Camp, regarded as the father of college football rules and one of the most credible authorities of the game during the era, chose to announce an All-Service team which would be announced at the end of the season in Collier's Weekly. Other organizations did name college All-America teams.

A major concern that attracted Heisman's attention in the weeks before the new season was that of player safety.

FOOTBALL DEATHS

Between 1910 and 1916 eighty athletes were reported to have died from football injuries. Seventeen of those were college players. The number of serious injuries recorded during the period were in the hundreds. The Associated Press reported a dozen football player deaths in 1917. All were college athletes except for one high school player.

The often regarded terse coach, who would not tolerate less than one hundred percent effort from his athletes, cared greatly for their well-being. This concern was first noted when Heisman urged Camp to endorse and add the forward pass to the rules of the game. Heisman believed too many players were getting hurt because there was no option other than running the ball to advance it down the field.

Keeping abreast of trends in the game, Heisman had heard of new head gear worn by football players that provided an additional safety feature to help reduce the number of head injuries.

In 1917 football helmets were redesigned to include a padded cradle in the top center of the helmet which provided space between the skull and the helmet. Fabric straps formed the cradle which helped protect players by absorbing and distributing the impact created from direct collisions. The new design also allowed better ventilation.

Heisman was aware of the new design during its early stages by sports industry giants Rawlings and Spalding. When the season began, he made sure his players were wearing the safer gear.

Getting Penn to Atlanta

Heisman had lined up nine opponents for the 1917 season including three perennial powers from the South and one anchor from the Ivy League, Pennsylvania.

Scheduling Pennsylvania was an out-of-the box strategic move by the Tech coach. If Georgia Tech was going to get the recognition it deserved, it was going to have earn its way by playing schools firmly embedded in the top of college football hierarchy. Heisman resolved that Tech could keep the schedule it had been playing for the past several years, win eight or nine games each year, and still not receive consideration as a nominee for a national championship.

He chose to recruit his alma mater Pennsylvania as Georgia Tech's resume builder. It was a good choice for a variety of reasons.

Pennsylvania possessed a football tradition as sacred as Dartmouth, Princeton and Harvard and attracted an impressive army of national sports writers that followed its games each Saturday. Penn began attracting the eyes of the national media and the nation's passionate football audience in the mid-1890s when George Woodruff held the reins as the university's football coach. From 1894–1898 Woodruff lost only two games and racked up 67 victories. His tenure at Penn served to put this university above all others in the Ivy League for a lengthy stretch of time.

Penn's success was highlighted again in the 1916 season under first-year head coach Bob Folwell when the squad posted a record of 7–2–1 and made a Rose Bowl appearance against Oregon.

Although Pennsylvania lost 14–0, Coach Folwell and his Quakers were still touted by the national press as a one of the finest college football programs in the land.

Transportation from Philadelphia to Atlanta was no easy matter. The Penn team would have to travel by rail more than 800 miles, a 26-hour excursion. Any way it was diced the trip to

Atlanta would take two days each way. If Penn was to arrive on the Friday before the Saturday game, the traveling party could be away from campus for as many as five days.

Heisman called on old friends, fellow alums, administrators he had known during his time at Penn and even some members of the press, including Grantland Rice, to persuade the Quakers that playing Tech in Atlanta could be a monumental event for the sport.

Penn took the bait, and the match was set for Saturday, October 6, almost a year to the day that Tech had swamped Cumberland 222–0.

The other eight

Besides Pennsylvania, the Georgia Tech schedule included Furman, Wake Forest, Davidson, Washington and Lee, Vanderbilt, Tulane, Carlisle and Auburn.

The collection of opponents who would begin play against Georgia Tech in late September was not necessarily a bastion of college football's best. But the game with Penn was a must in

POINT-A-MINUTE

Vanderbilt Coach Dan McGugin in his 14th year at the Nashville university in 1917 was being compared, mostly in newspapers in the South, as another John Heisman because of his offense's propensity to score points. In the seasons before playing Tech in 1917 Vanderbilt had an accomplished record of 16-2-1, which ranked among the best in the South and nationwide. In 1915 McGugin's Commodores scored 514 points in 510 minutes of playing time earning them the title the "Point-A-Minute" team.

order for Heisman to have a shot at his goal of a national championship crown.

Excluding Pennsylvania, the remaining eight opponents listed against Tech in 1917 had a combined record the previous year of 35–22–6.

The three strongest teams on the schedule besides Penn were Washington and Lee, Vanderbilt, and Auburn.

Reaching beyond Penn and Vanderbilt the next greatest threat facing Heisman's Engineers in his championship campaign would likely come from Washington and Lee. The Generals, as Vanderbilt, had been winning consistently for the past several years and perhaps more importantly, due to its location in Lexington, Virginia, a bit farther north than many of the teams considered in the Deep South, its football schedule frequently included teams on the watch lists of many of the major sports writers.

Washington and Lee finished the 1916 season 5–2–2, which included a win over Navy and ties against Georgia Tech and Army. The Generals were expected to be every bit as good in 1917.

Coach Heisman would place a checkmark beside Washington and Lee's name on the schedule tacked to the wall in his office as a reminder that this team could be the one to spoil the apple cart.

Auburn, too, earned a checkmark as a team of which to be wary. A team with three nicknames, War Eagles, Tigers and Plainsmen, Auburn had posted an exceptional 44–8–3 record dating back to 1910. That included an undefeated 8–0 season in 1913 and an 8–0–1 run in 1914. Going into the 1917 season it had been 11 years since Auburn had seen a losing season.

Heisman had good reason to believe the War Eagles would be formidable this fall.

Engineers report in mid-August

Heisman's 1917 squad began reporting in mid-August. Practice sessions were as serious as games to the coach. Before classes would begin around the second week in September,

Heisman ran his team through drills twice and sometimes three times a day. Practices were lengthy, punishing and exhaustive.

When the players weren't bumping heads in the ninety-degree-plus Georgia heat, they were sitting in a classroom, almost as hot as outside, bending an ear to Heisman lectures about what makes good football players and great football teams.

Twelve years before his reign at Tech, Heisman had been criticized for his locker-room antics and coaching style at Auburn. He was said to be overbearing and that his authoritarian demand for perfection was not effective, although others claimed that his lack of success at Auburn was primarily because of the woeful talent with which he had to work.

Heisman did not change. He continued to preach perfection and demand that his players think as they play the game. His team would hear the same speeches repeatedly.

This, he told his charges, had every promise of being a golden season for the Golden Tornado. He insisted on no uncertain terms that the 1917 college championship was theirs for the taking.

Opening weekend

The first two games of Georgia Tech's 1917 nine-game schedule were to be played on consecutive days in late September. They would be the season openers against independents Furman and Wake Forest. The Furman game was set for Friday, September 28, and Wake Forest, the stronger of the two, would tangle with them on early Saturday afternoon.

The arrangement for the two games made for an interesting quirk, although not foreign in the early years of college football. Schools would line up games on consecutive days for a variety of factors.

Heisman began his championship march with two resounding wins. Tech scored 58 points and did not allow their opponents a single crossing of the goal line. The Golden Tornado blanked Furman 25–0 and Wake Forest 33–0.

THREE BIG WINS IN FIVE DAYS

In 1903, the year Cumberland University and Clemson, which was coached at the time by John Heisman, were name co-champions of the Southern Intercollegiate Athletic Association, Cumberland pulled off three major victories in a five-day span.

Traveling to meeting their opponents on their own home turf, Cumberland beat Alabama 44–0 on November 14, in Tuscaloosa, Alabama; LSU 41–0 in Baton Rouge, Louisiana, two days later on November 16, and Tulane 28–0 in New Orleans on November 18. Cumberland ended its season with a tie against Clemson in a post-season bowl game. The Bulldogs only loss, a 6–0 decision, came at the hands of Sewanee. All of Cumberland's games in 1903 were played at the home stadiums of their opponents except for the bowl game against Clemson, an 11–11 tie, played in Montgomery, Ala. For the season Cumberland's stone wall defense held opponents scoreless except for Sewanee and Clemson.

Up next was the game that Heisman knew would either break or significantly enhance Tech's opportunity for a national championship. His engineers would face a capable Pennsylvania team that would bring with it to Grant Field all the aura and pomp associated with Ivy League football.

The event was far more than another game. It was an uncivil war that pitted the South against the Northeast.

Heisman recognized a win could be the single most important factor to get schools located outside the Northeast the credit they deserved.

Heisman's Golden Tornado pounced on Penn, scoring 41 points while holding the Quakers scoreless.

The New York Times pitched its story about the Atlanta massacre with the headline "Georgia Tech Yellow Jackets Rip Pennsy To Ribbons."

The Times reported "Strupper, Guyon and Hill smashed through the line at will, the first named reeling off a 70-yard run in the first three minutes of play for the first touchdown of the game. These three backs carried the brunt of the Yellow Jacket attack and they performed their Duties nobly."

"There was little doubt as to who would win the game after the first few minutes of play," said The Times, "and it was then only a question of the size of the score."

The Florida Times-Union, speaking for the South, praised Tech for its win and Heisman's coaching, adding that teams in the North in the future will have to "reckon with some of those of Dixieland."

The Times-Union described the results of the game as a "pleasant surprise."

Giving credit to the Yellow Jackets, the Jacksonville newspaper wrote that the unanticipated win by such a large margin over a football power from the North "was certainly furnished by the gridiron gladiators of Georgia Tech last Saturday when they defeated the eleven of the University of Pennsylvania by the decisive score of 41–0. Even the alumni of the Atlanta institution were amazed at the lopsided score. The result not only proves that Coach Heisman, despite his many handicaps, has built up a wonderful machine, but demonstrates that the large Eastern colleges will have to reckon with some of those of Dixieland in the future."

It was a new day for football in the South. John Heisman had proven to the world that football in the South was equal to or better than anywhere else in the country. The praise began to rain upon the crafty coach.

"I was present last Saturday and witnessed the North go down to your wonderful team. It verifies what I have long believed—that the South can produce as fine athletic men and as fine team work as the North in spite of the fact that we have not as much cool weather in which to drill our football material," wrote President W.L. Pickard of Mercer in a congratulatory letter to Heisman following the game.

Vanderbilt's Dan McGugin offered, "I take my pen in hand to congratulate Georgia Tech. You have certainly given an air of respectability to Southern football."

Accolades continued to pour in for the Yellow Jackets and their leader.

The defeat of Penn was a huge step for Tech on its road to a national championship but one giant leap for football in the South.

Never again would Southern football be a step-sister to the North or Northeast. Thanks to John Heisman and his Golden Tornado, football in the South had found its place on the national stage.

The season was not finished. Six games remained on the Tech schedule, and several posed major threats to upend and wreck Heisman's championship quest.

Next for Tech

Tech's dismantling of Pennsylvania made the Yellow Jackets the lead sports story in every major daily newspaper in America.

In their coverage of Heisman's team, many of the sports writers referred to the previous year when Tech had scored 222 points against Cumberland, although they didn't share nitty-gritty details of Heisman holding Cumberland's feet to the fire over the matter of money.

The nation's press hinted that it saw the rise of Tech coming almost exactly one year ago. Some had the opinion that the

KIND WORDS FROM AN OLD FRIEND

"Coach J.W. Heisman, of Georgia Tech, left Pennsylvania seventeen years ago.

"After an interval of seventeen years, he leads a lusty young arrival against his old university and finishes out in front, 41–0.

"Heisman stands as the prophet of the open game. The forward pass came in around 1906. Heisman was advocating this addition to the offence before 1900.

"Years before 1906 he had used lateral and other passes in profusion. The Tech coach has always been a great believer in the open game as against mass play. He has developed a greater variety of open field work than any football instructor in the realm, north, east, south or west. Many of these formations have failed to hold up against a charging defense. But many have proved bewildering and baffling.

"Winning Football elevens are nothing new in Heisman's life. He had great machines at Auburn back around 1898 and 1899; the same at Clemson, around 1901 and 1902, before Georgia Tech secured his services over twelve years ago," wrote Grantland Rice in The New York Tribune following the Penn game.

lopsided match was the key opening the nation's eyes to the strength of football in the South.

The game following Penn would be against a mediocre Davidson team, but Heisman was thinking a team with mediocre capacity still might get lucky and knock them from their perch.

He also worried that the hype in the press might affect his players in such a way as to make them overconfident and complacent about Saturday's match-up.

Davidson arrived in Atlanta with two losses.

Overcoming his concerns, Tech performed up to expectation with a convincing 32–10 win over the Wildcats. The coach was pleased but not overly so. His offense had played well but the defense had given up its first points of the season.

The game, like the Penn affair the week before, had attracted a covey of sports writers. They had returned to Atlanta for a different reason on this occasion. The previous week they had come to see what they figured was going to be a blowout of a team from the North over a team from the South. This week they had traveled to Atlanta to pinch themselves and to make sure what they had seen the week before was for real. They were satisfied.

Two powers in view

Preparing for games five and six, Heisman saw two teams with respectable football histories. Both Washington and Lee and Vanderbilt had fielded competitive teams in recent years, some of championship quality.

In the past ten years Georgia Tech had played Vanderbilt twice and Washington and Lee once. Heisman's recollection of all three games was very clear. He had not won a one of them.

In 1907 Vanderbilt crushed Tech 54–0 and three years later beat the Yellow Jackets 23–0. Both games were played in Atlanta.

Heisman remembered that his Engineers would have had a perfect season last year if it had not been for a 7–7 tie in the middle part of the Tech schedule with Washington and Lee. The Generals had been a formidable opponent the year before, and Heisman expected them to be up to the challenge again.

Since 1910, the Washington and Lee Generals had gone 45–10–5. They had managed consecutive winning seasons for nine straight years and were on track to repeat again in 1917. In 1914 Washington and Lee registered a perfect 9–0 season.

Vanderbilt's record since 1910 was 52–14–2. The Commodores had lodged only one losing season during the stretch, a 2–6 measure in 1914. In 1910 Vanderbilt had no losses and a tie for an 8–0–1 run, and in four other years during the period they managed to finish their seasons with only one loss. The Commodores had won three games and had lost one going into the 1917 game against Tech.

Tech tears into Washington and Lee

Tech rolled over Washington and Lee 63–0, and the next week slammed Vanderbilt 83–0, one of the Commodores worst defeats ever.

The Engineers now had played six games, scored 145 points, and allowed only 10 points.

Life is grand

With three games left the Yellow Jackets had become the talk of the nation. Each of their Saturday afternoon contests were being covered in detail by sports writers with the largest circulations in America.

There was jubilation in the South. Georgia Tech's campus buzzed with excitement. Atlanta was glowing, and the nation had a new team for whom to root in the heart of Dixie.

Clean sweep

Heisman keeping his team in gear swept the final three games with flash and fury.

With a take-no-prisoner mindset Georgia Tech beat Tulane in New Orleans 48–0 on November 10. Then returned home to devastate Carlisle 98–0, and closed the season by shutting down Auburn 68–7.

National champions

For the season Tech scored 491 points and allowed 17. Only Davidson and Auburn scored against the Golden Tornado. They averaged beating their opponents 55–2, playing eight games at home on Grant Field and one away in New Orleans against Tulane.

Shortly after the final whistle had blown reports of the Tech win over Auburn were racing across the country.

Four New York newspapers had a long tradition of anointing national champions from the North with little regard for schools in the South. Reluctantly, each named Georgia Tech as the finest team in the land.

The New York Times deliberated over the matter for weeks after Tech's final game before giving in and joining the others to declare the Yellow Jackets the best college football had to offer.

Georgia Tech even received an endorsement for the championship from one of its most fierce rivals, the University of Georgia.

The Red & Black, Georgia's campus newspaper, offered congratulations to the Yellow Jackets saying "Our hats go off to the 'Golden Tornado,' the wonderful eleven from Georgia Tech."

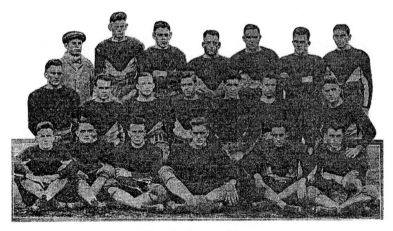

Tech's 1917 championship team

NEWSPAPER REPORTS

It was a given that newspapers in the South, in cities like Birmingham, Nashville, Savannah, and Atlanta, would endorse Georgia Tech as college football's best in 1917, but somewhat surprising were the positive reviews that came from several newspapers in the North particularly in New York.

The New York Sun wrote "Georgia Tech looms up as one of the truly great teams of all time. Football, once an Eastern specialty, now is a national sport, and in recognition of that we are glad to acclaim Georgia Tech the greatest eleven in the country."

The New York Evening Mail penned "Georgia Tech stands revealed as the most sensational football eleven of the year. There is no question about it. The University of Pittsburgh, Ohio State, and Minnesota have great football teams this year. But the record of the Golden Tornado of Atlanta is a bit beyond that of all of them."

The New York Globe announced "The one spike needed to clinch Georgia Tech's claim to the war-time Football championship of the universe was driven home on Thursday when the Yellow Jackets smothered Auburn under a 68–7 reckoning."

The New York Times called Tech a "football machine proclaimed by competent observers as the greatest Team which has ever been developed in the South and which was unquestionably the leading eleven of the last season."

The congratulations from Georgia did not come easy for two reasons; first, because of the bitter rivalry between the two schools, and secondly, because Georgia had not fielded a football team in 1917 due to the war in Europe. In 1917 and 1918 Georgia omitted football because of the war, while Tech's football program continued.

Wrap-up of 1917 season

Eighty-eight colleges and universities competed on the gridiron nationwide in 1917. It was a season that saw several schools suspend football in patriotic reverence to blood being shed by American soldiers on battlefields in Europe.

For John Heisman and his Golden Tornado the season was absolutely perfect, no losses, no ties, and a collection of thrilling wins.

For football in the South it was a renaissance of sorts.

Chants of a Civil War fought 50 years earlier and remembrances of General Sherman's torching of Atlanta had long passed. Cotton may no longer have been king, but for the first time ever there reigned a national collegiate football champion from the South.

Other college programs that fared well in 1917 and ended the season with a high ranking included Pittsburgh, 10–0; Ohio State, 8–0–1; Michigan, 8–2; and Georgetown, 8–1.

Pittsburgh would likely have been chosen the 1917 national champion if Georgia Tech had not beaten Pennsylvania so badly. That 41–0 romp was far more demonstrative of its superiority and position atop the heap of college football's best compared to Pitt's narrow 14–6 margin over the same Penn team.

Although the "dopesters," as one New York newspaper tagged the sports writers with the self-appointed duty to name a national champion, would have preferred to name Pittsburgh, they found they couldn't justify such a declaration.

Tech's championship team

Heisman's best squad since coming to Tech in 1904 was comprised of 21 players, a relatively small platoon. Fifteen of the athletes were from Georgia, and ten of the starters hailed from Georgia high schools.

Everett Strupper, Walker Carpenter, and Joe Guyon were named All-Americans, the first players to receive such honors from the Deep South. Strupper was a consensus pick.

Heisman ran what was recognized at the time as a "jump shift" offense in which three running backs (two halfbacks and a fullback) would line-up in an "I" formation stacked one behind the other. The three backs would shift to one side, the ball would be snapped, and they would explode forward into the defense providing a penetrating blocking force.

The national championship was celebrated by the Yellow Jackets at a special dinner held at Atlanta's Druid Hills Country Club on December 8. Each player received a commemorative gold football inscribed with the words "National Champions."

In later years Heisman claimed the 1917 team as the best he ever coached.

"It's the best team I have seen in my long career as a coach. I was lucky in having under me a team whose members possessed much natural ability and who played the game intelligently. I have never seen a team that, as a whole, was so fast in the composite," he said in describing his Golden Tornado fleet.

Members of that hallowed team, their hometowns and the position they played were: Si Bell, Orchard Hill, Georgia, end; Walker Carpenter, Newnan, Georgia, tackle; Alton Colcord, Atlanta, Georgia, end; Ham Dowling, Savannah, Georgia, guard; Bill Fincher, Spring Place, Georgia, tackle, end, guard, and center; Shorty Guill, Sparta, Georgia, end and fullback; Joe "O-Gee-Chidah" Guyon, White Earth, Minnesota, halfback; Judy Harlan, Ottumwa, Iowa, fullback; William Higgins, Roswell, New Mexico, tackle and guard; Albert Hill, Washington, Georgia, quarterback;

Charles Johnson, Atlanta, Georgia, end; Clarke Mathes, Jonesboro, Georgia, guard; Pup Phillips, Carnesville, Georgia, center; J.R. Rogers, Memphis, Tennessee, tackle and guard; Theodore Shaver, Dayton, Georgia, halfback; Everett Strupper, Columbus, Georgia, halfback; William Thweatt, Pope, Mississippi, tackle and guard; Ray Ulrich, Chicago, Illinois, end; Dan Whelchel, Ashburn, Georgia, tackle and guard; William Simpson, Atlanta, Georgia, running back; and Wally Smith, Atlanta, Georgia, running back.

CHAPTER
SIXTEEN

WHAT
FOLLOWS

The next year, 1918

Although the 1918 Georgia Tech team came nowhere near to resembling the 1917 national championship squad, the Golden Tornado remained in the news, still attracting headlines on sports pages across America.

Many on Tech's championship team left school at the end of the season to represent America on battlefronts in Europe during World War I.

That meant it was going to be a challenging season for the man behind the clipboard regarded as one of the best minds to have coached the game.

Sportswriters, especially from the North, were watching Heisman and his Engineers closely. Columns appeared in newspapers nationwide pondering if Tech could repeat in 1918.

Tech reeled off five straight wins scoring more than 100 points in three of the games while its defense did not relinquish a single point. Playing the first five games at home Heisman's team beat Clemson, 28–0; Furman, 118–0; the 11th Cavalry, 123–0; Camp Gordon, 28–0; and North Carolina State, 128–0.

Game six required Heisman and his Yellow Jackets to travel north and play a nationally ranked Pittsburgh team coached by the legendary Pop Warner.

Both teams were undefeated when they met on November 23, although Pitt, playing a somewhat abbreviated schedule, had only two games under its belt after beating Washington and Jefferson 34–0 and Pennsylvania 37–0.

If Tech could win at Pitt, Heisman would likely be picking up his second national championship, but the offense could not get on track. Pitt's defense was stifling, and the Panthers offense streaked through gaps in the Yellow Jackets defense.

The game's ending proved disappointing for Coach Heisman. His trek to a second national championship was derailed. Pittsburgh won 32–0.

Despite Pitt's season being cut short because of the Spanish Flu pandemic (five games were eliminated from the schedule), the Panthers went 4–1 and were named the 1918 national football champions. Tech finished 1918 with a 41–0 win over Auburn and a record of 6–1.

War touches all

World War I had a crippling effect on college enrollment as well as football.

Young men who were ripe for the game in 1917 and 1918 were in the sights of Army and Marine recruiters. Appealing to their emotions to fight in a war to end all wars, many who should have been on their way to enroll in college and report for fall football practice enlisted and reported for basic training.

About a dozen from Georgia Tech's championship team, feeling the need to answer the call of patriotic duty, enlisted in the military and were off to war.

It was no different for Georgia Tech than for Pennsylvania, Pittsburgh, Ohio State, or Cumberland University.

The war decimated Cumberland's enrollment from 1917 to 1919. In 1917 the law school conferred degrees on 82 students including most of those who had made the trip to Atlanta the previous fall to play Tech.

By January 1918 the number of law graduates had dwindled to sixteen. In June the university handed out degrees to thirty-eight, less than half the number who had graduated the year before. Outside of the law school, there were only a couple of dozen students in the college who graduated in 1918.

The war had taken its toll on this small private university in Middle Tennessee that depended on tuition fees for financial stability.

Cumberland reboots football, again

Cumberland University's football program before and following the bout with Georgia Tech had been an on-and-off-again experience. Before disbanding football in the spring of 1916, Cumberland had quit and resumed the sport twice before.

When World War I ended on the 11th hour of the 11th day of November 1918, peace was restored to the world.

One of the aftereffects was that college enrollment surged, and as campuses swelled with young military veterans, college football received a shot in the arm, and the excitement about the game was reignited.

Following a four-year hiatus after the Georgia Tech game, Cumberland resumed football in the autumn of 1920. The university competed on the gridiron for the following ten years until the onset of the Great Depression in 1929 once again forced the administration to drop the sport as the school had its hands full simply keeping afloat as an educational institution.

However, three years later Cumberland fielded a team and joined the Smokey Mountain Athletic Conference. The university immediately found success in the sport winning conference championships in 1932, 1933, 1934, and 1935.

Schools that competed in the conference included Tennessee Technological University, Middle Tennessee State Teachers College (Middle Tennessee State University), Carson Newman, Tampa, Sewanee, and Appalachian State.

During this stretch Cumberland maintained a football program for ten seasons, dropping its program in 1941 and picking it back up in 1947 two years after the conclusion of World War II.

A shining and most memorable victory for Cumberland came in the 1947 season when the Bulldogs managed a 6–0 win over Florida State. Following the 1949 season, Cumberland exited the sport again and did not field another team until 1990 when it began competing in the National American

Intercollegiate Association (NAIA), which is where the school still competes today.

No luck

Two years after winning the national championship, Coach Heisman was as popular as ever in Atlanta. His Golden Tornado was still winning and still viable as a contender for national championship titles.

The 1919 season began with five straight victories. And just as in past seasons, Heisman's offense was ripping up and down the field plastering the scoreboard with points, while the defense blanked their opponents.

Through the first five games the Yellow Jackets scored 184 points. Tech beat Furman 74–0 and then posted wins over Wake Forest, Vanderbilt and Clemson, three solid programs in the South. The ground work had been laid for another run at a national championship.

John Heisman's name had become as familiar to America as Coca-Cola, Wrigley's Chewing Gum, and Borax soap, and, after proving himself and the credibility of football in the South, he and his Golden Tornado nurtured a sweetheart relationship with the national press.

Sports writers had come to the realization that football in the South was every bit as potent as football at Pittsburgh, Pennsylvania, Ohio State, Dartmouth or Harvard.

The sixth game on the 1918 schedule would take Tech away from the comfortable environment of Grant Field to face another powerful Pittsburgh Panthers squad. Pittsburgh was 2–1 going into the Tech game with a 24–3 loss to Syracuse. Pittsburgh had a good team but was not considered in the hunt for a national title.

Pitt surprised Tech, odds-makers, and most of the nation as it overtook the Yellow Jackets, 16–6.

Tech wound up the 1919 campaign losing three of its final five games, finishing 7–3.

Key administrators on campus were confident Heisman would get things back in order for the next year and that Tech would reassume its place among college football's elite.

An erroneous forecast

With the season done, there were matters that needed to be cleared up such as attendance records, accounting of travel expenses, storing of equipment and uniforms, and final arrangements for the 1920 schedule.

Business around Heisman's office seemed normal. There was chatter about next year, about which players would be returning, and about whom might start at the most important positions.

Nothing seemed out of the ordinary, until members of the Georgia Tech athletic board received a telephone call from their coach, inviting them to his home for a private conversation.

When the group arrived they found Heisman and his wife sitting solemnly at the breakfast table.

Coach Heisman began to explain that he and Mrs. Heisman had been dealing with a troubled marriage for several months. They had reached the decision that it would be best for them to divorce.

He insisted that the separation was amicable, and that they had agreed that because it would be socially awkward that it would be best for both if they lived in separate cities.

The coach had concluded that it would be his wife's decision to decide where she would make her home, and he would live elsewhere.

Evelyn Heisman declared she would remain in Atlanta.

Coach Heisman's immediate resignation shocked the collegiate football world. The school where he had been so successful, where he had etched an extraordinary winning record of 102–29–7 and had won a national football championship, would no longer own his heart, soul and mind.

Accepting the head coaching position at his alma mater, the University of Pennsylvania, he almost immediately left Atlanta for Philadelphia.

Struggles ahead

After his sixteen-year stint in Atlanta Heisman's woes began to mount. His move to Pennsylvania became a matter of turmoil exaggerated by a 16–10–2 record at Penn.

His players grew exasperated with his Shakespearean lock-er-room orations and proved lackadaisical during practice and performed likewise on game days. The athletes were dissatisfied with their coach as he was with them.

The opportunity availed for Heisman to take a coaching post at Washington and Jefferson, a small liberal arts college in Washington, Penn. Concerned about the unstable environment at his alma mater, the mindset of his Quaker players, and what seemed to him to be their disdain for his coaching methodology, he departed Philadelphia and accepted the job at Washington and Jefferson.

After a one-year hitch and a 6–1–1 record, he moved Southwest to Rice University.

Heisman's migration to Rice was motivated to some degree by a large salary increase. Serving as head football coach and athletic director, he was paid more than any other faculty member at Rice.

While on the Houston, Texas, campus he became reacquainted with Edith Cole, a former Buchtel College co-ed with whom he had shared a romantic relationship while coaching at the small college in Akron, Ohio, 30 years earlier. The two married in 1924.

Heisman struggled at Rice for four years. In 1927, his final season to coach, his Owls won two games, lost six and tied one. It was a dismal record, his worst at Rice and the worst in his long coaching career. During his first coaching stop west of the

Mississippi and for the first time as a head coach, John Heisman lost more games than he won, finishing with a 14–18–3 record.

At age 58, John Heisman was done drawing Xs and Os. He was leaving the coaching profession.

On to New York City

After turning in his resignation at Rice, Heisman and his mate moved to New York where he wrote a sports column for *Collier's* magazine and became the managing director of the New York City Downtown Athletic Club. He soon introduced the idea to the club that they present an annual trophy to college football's most outstanding player.

The members agreed and created a trophy to recognize the best college football player east of the Mississippi River. The recipient of the first award in 1935 was Jay Berwanger, an outstanding halfback for the University of Chicago.

Then, on October 3, 1936, John Heisman died in New York City twenty days before his sixty-seventh birthday, succumbing to a short bout with pneumonia.

The trophy

After Heisman's death the club chose to name the award in his honor and the scope of nominations was broadened to include all of the United States.

Today the Heisman Trophy is presented to the most outstanding player in college football whose performance best exhibits the pursuit of excellence with integrity. Recipients of the award are to have demonstrated superior ability on the gridiron and exhibited character traits practiced by its namesake including diligence, perseverance, and hard work. The award is presented annually in December by the Heisman Trophy Trust.

HEISMAN TROPHY WINNERS:

1935	Jay Berwanger	Chicago	Halfback
1936	Larry Kelley	Yale	End
1937	Clint Frank	Yale	Halfback
1938	Davey O'Brien	TCU	Quarterback
1939	Nile Kinnick	Iowa	Halfback/Quarterback
1940	Tom Harmon	Michigan	Halfback
1941	Bruce Smith	Minnesota	Halfback
1942	Frank Sinkwich	Georgia	Halfback
1943	Angelo Bertelli	Notre Dame	Quarterback
1944	Les Horvath	Ohio State	Halfback/Quarterback
1945	Doc Blanchard	Army	Fullback
1946	Glenn Davis	Army	Halfback
1947	Johnny Lujack	Notre Dame	Quarterback
1948	Doak Walker	SMU	Halfback
1949	Leon Hart Notre	Dame	End
1950	Vic Janowicz	Ohio State	Halfback/Punter
1951	Dick Kazmaier	Princeton	Halfback
1952	Billy Vessels	Oklahoma	Halfback
1953	Johnny Lattner	Notre Dame	Halfback
1954	Alan Ameche	Wisconsin	Fullback
1955	Howard Cassady	Ohio State	Halfback
1956	Paul Hornung	Notre Dame	Quarterback
1957	John David Crow	Texas A&M	Halfback
1958	Pete Dawkins	Army	Halfback
1959	Billy Cannon	LSU	Halfback
1960	Joe Bellino	Navy	Halfback
1961	Ernie Davis	Syracuse	Halfback/Linebacker/Fullback
1962	Terry Baker	Oregon State	Quarterback
1963	Roger Staubach	Navy	Quarterback
1964	John Huarte	Notre Dame	Quarterback
1965	Mike Garrett	USC	Halfback
1966	Steve Spurrier	Florida	Quarterback
1967	Gary Beban	UCLA	Quarterback
1968	O.J. Simpson	USC	Halfback
1969	Steve Owens	Oklahoma	Fullback
1970	Jim Plunkett	Stanford	Quarterback
1971	Pat Sullivan	Auburn	Quarterback
1972	Johnny Rodgers	Nebraska	Wide Receiver/Running Back
1973	John Cappelletti	Penn State	Running Back

Continued

1974	Archie Griffin	Ohio State	Running Back
1975	Archie Griffin	Ohio State	Running Back
1976	Tony Dorsett	Pittsburgh	Running Back
1977	Earl Campbell	Texas	Running Back
1978	Billy Simms	Oklahoma	Running Back
1979	Charles White	USC	Running Back
1980	George Rogers	South Carolina	Running Back
1981	Marcus Allen	USC	Running Back
1982	Herschel Walker	Georgia	Running Back
1983	Mike Rozier	Nebraska	Running Back
1984	Doug Flutie	Boston College	Quarterback
1985	Bo Jackson	Auburn	Running Back
1986	Vinny Testaverde	Miami	Quarterback
1987	Tim Brown	Notre Dame	Wide Receiver
1988	Barry Sanders	Oklahoma State	Running Back
1989	Andre Ware	Houston	Quarterback
1990	Ty Detmer	BYU	Quarterback
1991	Desmond Howard	Michigan	Wide Receiver/Punt Returner
1992	Gino Torretta	Miami	Quarterback
1993	Charlie Ward	Florida State	Quarterback
1994	Rashaan Salaam	Colorado	Running Back
1995	Eddie George	Ohio State	Running Back
1996	Danny Wuerffel	Florida	Quarterback
1997	Charles Woodson	Michigan	Cornerback/Punt Returner
1998	Ricky Williams	Texas	Running Back
1999	Ron Dayne	Wisconsin	Running Back
2000	Chris Weinke	Florida State	Quarterback
2001	Eric Crouch	Nebraska	Quarterback
2002	Carson Palmer	USC	Quarterback
2003	Jason White	Oklahoma	Quarterback
2004	Matt Leinart	USC	Quarterback
2005 (Vacated)	Reggie Bush	USC	Running Back
2006	Troy Smith	Ohio State	Quarterback
2007	Tim Tebow	Florida	Quarterback
2008	Sam Bradford	Oklahoma	Quarterback
2009	Mark Ingram Jr.	Alabama	Running Back
2010	Cam Newton	Auburn	Quarterback
2011	Robert Griffin III	Baylor	Quarterback
2012	Johnny Manziel	Texas A&M	Quarterback
2013	Jameis Winston	Florida State	Quarterback
2014	Marcus Mariota	Oregon	Quarterback
2015	Derrick Henry	Alabama	Running Back

Selection process

The selection of the Heisman Trophy winner each year is determined by a collection of votes from three independent constituencies including sports journalists (870 media votes, 145 votes from each of six regions), previous winners of the trophy, and, added to the selection process most recently, a compilation of votes from fans of football in cooperation with the ESPN television network.

The third element for selecting a Heisman winner, which allows college football enthusiasts to participate, was introduced in 1999. The survey collected from college football fans is tallied and constitutes one vote in the Heisman election. Fans cast their respective votes online at ESPN.com.

Each person voting in the Heisman is asked to designate three selections ranking them in order of preference. In the process of totaling votes, each first place selection tallies three points, second place receives two points and third place gets one point.

Through 2015, Notre Dame and the University of Southern California share the distinction of having the most Heisman winners. Each has had seven players receive the trophy. Ohio State has had six winners; Oklahoma, five; and Army, Auburn, Florida, Florida State, Michigan, and Nebraska have had three each.

What if?

What if the 1916 game between Cumberland and Georgia Tech had never been played?

If George Allen hadn't rallied his fraternity brothers for the trip to Atlanta, it's likely Cumberland University would have faced bankruptcy and closed its doors.

The school was struggling financially at the time. To add an invoice for damages in a breach of contract claim by Coach John Heisman and Georgia Tech, paying up could have been devastating as the penalty would have amounted to more than $100,000 in today's monetary values.

Founded in 1842, Cumberland University continues today as an accredited four-year university with an enrollment of approximately 1,500.

If Heisman had acquiesced to Cumberland's request to let the small Tennessee university off the hook from playing Georgia Tech in Atlanta, his team would never have received the national spotlight for the 222 points with which his Engineers managed to dominate the scoreboard.

And likely the absence of that exposure by the nation's sports writing press corps would have severely crippled Georgia Tech's successful campaign the very next year to be named college football's national champion.

Heisman's insistence that the game be played, and his team's offensive dominance that allowed Tech to score at will not only captured the attention of football fans nationwide, it also caused a bevy of sports writers headquartered in the Northeast to look South and to realize for perhaps the first time that the sport in this region was being played with as much talent, enthusiasm, grit, and skill as in other parts of the country.

The gosh-almighty score, 222–0, opened doors for football in the South, making a dramatic statement. While Harvard, Dartmouth, Pittsburgh, and other schools in the Northeast had been the dominant headliners in the national press, the time had come to recognize the abilities of the teams playing the sport below the Mason-Dixon Line.

Even if the game had not been played, John Heisman still would have made his name as a football legend. His multiple contributions to the sport will be recognized for as long as the game is played. But the lopsided score his Tech team inflicted on Cumberland University is more than a simple asterisk in the record books.

As for George Allen, if the game in Atlanta had never occurred, his tenure at Cumberland would have come to the same conclusion.

He would have heard lecture upon lecture in law classes, partied at fraternity socials, been at the center of student life, and, after receiving his law degree, would still have been a successful attorney, political operative and advisor to four American presidents.

But he wouldn't have had the conversation with President Dwight Eisenhower on October 7, 1960, at Burning Tree Golf Club about what he was doing on the same day forty-four years earlier.

Four hours later

The fall afternoon sun is fading quickly. Both men by now have donned sweaters to counter a seasonal chill in the air encouraged by a slight northerly breeze.

After 17 holes George and the president were only separated by one stroke as they squared off on the 18th green.

Ike, boasting a 15 handicap at the time, was having a decent round. He was laying three on the par four hole with only a three foot putt remaining to closeout his round. If it sinks, he'll have an 83 for the day.

George, trailing by one stroke, but on the green in two has a chance to tie his friend and playing foe if he can hit a 12 footer for a birdie.

Surveying the route between him and the cup, George sees bumps and curves ahead. Meanwhile Ike is focused on his awaiting three foot strike.

"What I'm looking at here isn't so unlike the trip I took to Atlanta in 1916," George reckoned out loud to Ike as he continued to study his putt.

"I was facing all sorts of challenges, troubles you might say. There were nightmarish bumps in the road and curves thrown at me from every direction that I nor anyone else could see coming.

"I was relegated to but one option and that was to put a frat team of college boys together and make the trip south to Atlanta in order to save my university and probably save my own ass as it turned out.

"And here I am now, 44 years later, facing bumps in my way and breaks I can't see to save my ass once again," George said laughing a bit as he lowered his voice almost to a whisper before stroking his putt.

His ball began slowly meandering forward. It bumped and darted back and forth. As the ball got to within three feet of the hole, the president could see the putt was going to be good, and exclaimed, "By golly George you've done it again. You've saved your ass."

It wasn't the first time that this story teller, well spoken lawyer, politician and public servant had stepped up his game to achieve a heroic-like outcome.

But not on this day or for that matter any other day in his life had he produced results with such overwhelming consequences as he had in 1916.

"Pick it up," George instructed Ike declaring the president's remaining three footer a gimme.

"Let's go grab a Johnnie Walker Black and call it a day."

A life like few others

George Allen, the man who had personally served four U.S. presidents, been featured on the cover of Time magazine in 1946, and lived a life of charm died on April 27, 1973 at the age of 77.

In his lifetime he was able to see the world from both sides of the Atlantic, play a masterful role in national politics, rub elbows with the nation's elite and do a thousand things for which others could only dream.

George did all of this and also managed, as a young college student, to save a southern university from financial demise.

CUMBERLAND UNIVERSITY SPORTS HIGHLIGHTS

While Cumberland may be most recognized for the record-setting loss it suffered at the hands of Georgia Tech and John Heisman in 1916, there are numerous highlights in the university's sporting efforts.

In 1894 Cumberland University fielded its first football team.

In 1903 Cumberland beats Tulane, LSU, Alabama and the University of Tennessee at Chattanooga in a five-day road trip, scoring 250 points and skunking its opponents. Cumberland capped off the championship season with a post-season game, the first of its kind to be played in the South, against John Heisman's Clemson Tigers. The Thanksgiving Day game, played in Montgomery, Alabama, ended in an 11–11 tie.

In 1932, 1933, 1934, and 1935 Cumberland captured football championship titles in the Smokey Mountain Athletic Conference.

In 1947, Cumberland's football team defeated Florida State University 6–0.

Cumberland's baseball team made twelve appearances in the NAIA World Series, and in 2004, 2010, and 2014 won the national championship, all under the helm of Coach Woody Hunt.

Among those who have coached at Cumberland, one of the most outstanding in recent history is Cliff Ellis, who coached basketball

Continued

from 1972 to 1975 before leaving for coaching jobs at South Alabama (1975–1984), Clemson (1884–1994), Auburn (1994–2004) and now at Coastal Carolina.

While at Auburn Ellis was named National Coach of the Year in 1999 by the Associated Press. In 1995 and 1999 he received honors for Southeastern Conference Coach of the Year, and in 1987 and 1990 he was named Atlantic Coast Conference Coach of the Year.

ADDENDUM

40 years after the game

In 1956 at the suggestion of the Greater Atlanta Club, 28 participants of the 1916 game, including 22 former players from Tech and six from Cumberland, attended a special 40 year anniversary reunion to celebrate the historic event they made possible.

Gathering attention from members of the national press, the program which attracted more than 200 Georgia Tech alumni, was reported by newspapers from coast to coast.

George Griffin, who played in the game for Tech served as toastmaster for the event, while Tech's 1916 team captain, Talley Johnson, introduced the Tech players present.

Representing Cumberland, Gentry Dugat, also a player in the game, introduced attending former players from his alma mater as well as a couple of special guests including O.K. Armstrong, who had written a story about the game that was published in Reader's Digest.

The reunion provided a suitable venue for the former players to reminisce with each other and retell their personal accounts about arguably the most memorable football game ever played.

According to one report about the reunion published in Tech's Alumni Magazine, hearing game participants tell their own favorite anecdotes about the game was the most entertaining part of the event.

Cumberland's Morris Gouger, a Texas banker at the time of the reunion, entertained attendees with details about how the score could have even been worse.

"I called for a quarterback sneak on fourth down late in the final period," Gouger said. "We needed 25 yards and were deep in our territory. I made it back to the line of scrimmage and saved us from really ignominious defeat. If we had punted, as we should have, Tech would have blocked the kick, made another touchdown and the score would have been 229–0."

As first person accounts about the game continued, some in conflict with each other, one Tech alum is said to have lamented,

"This rematch is fixed. How do you expect 22 engineers to out talk six lawyers."

Several Tech players remembered that after the game Coach Heisman declared they had played a "fairly good game," but even so they were directed back to the practice field for what they described as a "vigorous 30-minute scrimmage."

They also remembered that Heisman had played his first and second teams in alternate quarters and had promised that the squad with the most points would be rewarded with a steak dinner. At the end of the day, after their scrimmage, they said their coach congratulated them and awarded all with a steak dinner that evening.

Dugat, addressing the audience offered, "Little did we realize we were playing ourselves into immortality that day. We made you of Georgia Tech a great team."

His observation, likely shared by all reunion attendees, was ever so true. Cumberland's 222–0 loss to Tech in 1916 set the stage for Tech's national championship the very next year.

45 years later Cumberland sells prestigious law school

In 1961, 45 years after the game was played in Atlanta, Cumberland University brokered a deal to sell its prestigious School of Law to Samford University in Birmingham, Ala. The transaction was closed and all assets of the law school were transferred to Samford in 1962 for a sum of $125,000.

The law school was overwhelmed with demands by the American Bar Association and other accrediting agencies to strengthen its law library and to add a great number of fulltime faculty members and additional administrators. The requirements proved to be too financially stringent on Cumberland and the school's Board of Trust voted to sell the once highly acclaimed School of Law to Samford.

This school, that provided the education for a former U.S. Secretary of State and founder of the United Nations, Cordell Hull;

two Justices of the U.S. Supreme Court; more than 82 members of the U.S. Congress; 16 state governors, and scores of members of the federal, state and local judiciary, closed its doors in Lebanon and sold the old "Law Barn," Caruthers Hall, which strongly favored Philadelphia's Independence Hall, to a local bank that years later tore down the structure opting for a modern contemporary styled building. It too was torn down by a second bank in order to build another more accommodating building.

A historical marker remains at the corner of West Main Street and North Greenwood in Lebanon noting that once on this property stood Caruthers Hall, the home of the Cumberland University School of Law.

From four year university to junior college to four year university

Believing Cumberland should find a new niche to meet current financial burdens in 1957, the school's Board of Trust opted to change the university's curriculum from a four year degree program to that of a two year associate's degree. Cumberland became a private, independent junior college and remained so for some 25 years.

In 1982 Cumberland's trustees voted to return the school to its original position as an accredited four year university.

Now accredited, as many other universities in the South by the Southern Association of Colleges and Schools, Cumberland offers a number of baccalaureate degree programs as well as graduate studies. Cumberland also maintains one of the state's outstanding nursing programs, the Dr. Jeanette C. Rudy School of Nursing.

Tech's best games on Grant Field

Georgia Tech has mastered and surprised a number of opponents on Grant Field since its opening in 1913. These may be the 12 best games.

October 7, 1916: Georgia Tech 222, Cumberland University 0

The game played to keep one school out of bankruptcy and the other, Georgia Tech, on a track to win a national championship. The score still remains as the largest victory in collegiate football ever.

November 29, 1917: Georgia Tech 68, Auburn 7

With this victory came the successful completion of the end of the first undefeated, untied National Championship season for the Yellow Jackets.

December 8, 1928: Georgia Tech 20, Georgia 6

This game concluded a second perfect season for Tech and another National Championship. The Yellow Jackets went on to beat Cal 8–7 in the Rose Bowl. Tech won nine consecutive games in the regular season topping the perfect stretch off with the Rose Bowl victory.

November 15, 1952: No. 4 Georgia Tech 7, No. 12 Alabama 3

In one of the biggest games of Georgia Tech's third National Championship season, two of the highest ranked teams to ever play on Grant Field saw Georgia Tech defeat Alabama in a closely matched defensive battle.

November 17, 1962: Georgia Tech 7, No. 1 Alabama 6

This incredible upset victory over top-ranked Alabama ended the Crimson Tide's 26-game unbeaten streak. Tech coach Bobby Dodd called it his greatest victory as Tech thwarted Alabama comeback efforts by preventing a two-point conversion attempt and intercepting a Joe Namath pass deep in their own territory with just 1:05 left.

November 6, 1976: Georgia Tech 23, No. 11 Notre Dame 14

In the most memorable game of a 4–6–1 season, Georgia Tech defeated #11 Notre Dame without throwing a forward pass.

October 13, 1990: No. 15 Georgia Tech 21, No. 14 Clemson 19

Only two seasons past a miserable 3–8 1988 season, Tech's Bobby Ross led his team to a 4–0 record to face the Tigers. The Yellow Jackets came out on top and went on to defeat No. 1 Virginia in the regular season and No.19 Nebraska in the Citrus Bowl to secure the school's fourth National Championship.

October 17, 1998: No. 25 Georgia Tech 41, No. 7 Virginia 38

It was the second meeting between two highly ranked Georgia Tech and Virginia teams (the first being in 1990). Georgia Tech won again and by the same score 41–38 earning the Yellow Jackets a share of the ACC Championship.

November 27, 1999: No. 16 Georgia Tech 51, No. 21 Georgia 48 (OT)

In the highest scoring game ever in the series with Georgia. The Bulldogs overcame a 17-point deficit in the second half to tie the game and appeared to be within easy victory after driving to Tech's 2-yard line with nine seconds left to play. Rather than kick a game winning field goal, Georgia coach Jim Donnan called a running play that was ruled a fumble that Georgia Tech recovered in the end zone. Tech attempted a field goal on third down in its possession. The kick was blocked, but the Tech holder recovered the ball. Tech succeeded on its second chance kick on fourth down and won the game.

November 1, 2008: Georgia Tech 31, No. 16 Florida State 28

Before the 2008 meeting between FSU and Georgia Tech, FSU's Bobby Bowden was undefeated against the Yellow Jackets. The last time Georgia Tech had defeated Florida State was in 1975. Bowden had never lost to Georgia Tech in 12 meetings.

October 17, 2009: No. 19 Georgia Tech 28, No. 4 Virginia Tech 23

Played before an emotionally charged crowd, this was the first time Georgia Tech defeated a top five team at home since beating No. 1 Alabama 7–6 in 1962.

October 29, 2011: Georgia Tech 31, No. 5 Clemson 17

Before a sellout crowd of 55,646, Georgia Tech rebounded from two consecutive losses to upset No. 5 Clemson.

Skirmish with Bear leads to SEC withdrawal

After the record setting win over Cumberland, after football gained credibility in the South largely because of the Cumberland game, and after Heisman's Engineers won a national title in 1917, Georgia Tech's reputation emerged nationally as a football powerhouse.

In 1932, 16 years after the Cumberland game, Georgia Tech and 12 other schools including Alabama, Auburn, Florida, Georgia, Kentucky, LSU, Mississippi, Mississippi State, Sewanee, Tennessee, Tulane and Vanderbilt, formed the Southeastern Conference.

Many believe Tech was persuaded to withdraw from the conference in 1963 during Coach Bobby Dodd's era as the result of a clash between Dodd and Alabama Coach Paul "Bear" Bryant involving a controversial hit made on a Tech player.

The incident happened in a game being played at Legion Field in Birmingham in 1961.

Tech had punted the ball to Alabama. The Crimson Tide player receiving the punt called for a "fair catch." Seeing the player receiving the punt waive for a "fair catch," Chick Graning, covering the punt for Tech, retreated from his charge toward the Alabama punt receiver and while in a somewhat defenseless position was hit with significant force from a Bama blocker.

Dodd believed the hit, which left Graning unconscious with a number of broken bones to his face, a broken nose and a severe concussion, was uncalled for. The hit was so severe that it ended Graning's football career.

Dodd, by a formal written letter, asked Bryant to suspend the player who he believed had intentionally inflicted injury on Graning. But Bryant refused to do so. Dodd became so angry over the matter that soon afterwards Tech began conversations about leaving the SEC. And in 1963 did so.

Incidentally, Alabama won that game by a 10–0 score and went on to win its first Associated Press National Championship the same year.

72 years after 222–0 game Tech adds Dodd's name to stadium

In 1988 the Georgia State Board of Regents voted to name the stadium surrounding Georgia Tech's Grant Field the Bobby Dodd Stadium in honor of another legendary Yellow Jackets coach.

The name change was the first for the Tech football facility since it was named Hugh Inman Grant Field in 1914 two years before the game with Cumberland.

Dodd coached at Tech from 1945 through 1966 compiling a record of 165–64–8. He also served as Georgia Tech's athletic director from 1951 to 1976 and afterwards as a consultant to the school's alumni association until his death in 1988. In all his term of service with Tech spanned more than 57 years.

Since Grant Field was built by students at the Institute just prior to 1905, the first season Tech played on the field, much has changed about this hallowed ground for Georgia Tech football and especially its unique location as it sits quietly, except on Saturday afternoons, among rising skyscrapers in downtown Atlanta. Bobby Dodd Stadium/Grant Field is located in the center of Tech's campus.

When Tech played Cumberland in 1916, the stadium at Grant Field could seat about 5,500. By 1925 the size of the stadium had been increased to a capacity of near 30,000. Since then several additions have been made to the stadium including a project in 1947 in which the West Stands were rebuilt adding about 10,000 seats and a new press box, and in 1958 when the North Stands were constructed increasing capacity to more than 44,000.

In 1962 a second deck was added to the East side that increased seating capacity to more than 53,000. The West Stands were double-decked in 1967 and the stadium's capacity was raised to 58,121. The stadium's current capacity is 55,000.

Two games have seen the stadium filled above capacity. In 1973 more than 60,000 watched a game between Tech and Georgia and in 2006 more than 58,000 fans crammed into the stadium to see the season opener between the Yellow Jackets and Notre Dame.

ADDENDUM

Coach Bobby Dodd

An outstanding college quarterback at the University of
Tennessee from 1928 to 1930 playing under legendary coach
Gen. Robert Neyland, Bobby Dodd took over as head foot-
ball coach at Georgia Tech in 1945 following Coach William
Alexander.

From Kingsport, Tenn., Dodd went 27–1–2 when starting at
quarterback for the Volunteers.

It was in 1930 in a game against Florida when Dodd displayed
a genius for creativity that would later serve to compliment his
portfolio as a college coach. Gathering his fellow players in the
huddle, Dodd began to describe a play he had once used in high
school. His instructions were to place the ball on the ground once
it had been snapped and to leave it there unattended and for all
players to run in one direction away from the ball. The center
was told circle back behind his teammates, pick-up the ball, and
head for the goal line. The play worked as planned and the center
waltzed into the end zone untouched.

Again the same play was used by Nebraska in the 1984
Orange Bowl against Miami and from that time forward the play
was recognized as the "fumblerooski."

Dodd became so popular at UT that the fans clad in orange
created a motto for his play that found its way into some cheers as
crowds would chant "In Dodd we trust."

Wally Butts, a longtime Head coach at Georgia, once
commenting on a reputation Dodd had for being lucky said "If
Bobby Dodd were trapped in the center of an H-Bomb explosion,
he'd walk away with his pockets full of marketable uranium."

About his luck Dodd responded, "Lucky. Bet your life I am
lucky. I'm lucky and so are my teams. It's a habit. You know, if you
think you're lucky you are."

Dodd left his head coaching position at Tech in 1967. He was
succeeded by Bud Carson.

Game ball auctioned

In 2014, 98 years after the historic match-up between Cumberland and Tech, the game ball used on that day was sold for $40,388 to Ryan Schneider, an Atlanta attorney and 1990 Tech graduate.

Schneider was named the successful bidder and awarded the ball after an online auction was conducted for almost three weeks.

Before the auction began it had been thought that the ball may bring as much as $5,000. One of the highest amounts to ever be paid for a game ball at the time was $26,046. The football in this case was signed by all members of the 1966 Green Bay Packers, winners of the first Super Bowl.

Schneider, who later said placing the winning bid was like "my red car for midlife crisis," gave the ball to Georgia Tech to be placed on display in the Institute's athletic department.

The ball was auctioned as a fund-raiser for the LA84 Foundation, a non-profit that funds youth sports in southern California. The foundation inherited it along with a vast collection of sports artifacts from a Los Angeles sports museum opened in the 1930's, the Helms Athletic Foundation. The ball had been donated to the museum by Bill Schroeder, an avid sports collector who was known to acquire items simply by writing to sports figures to ask for them. As the museum changed locations, the ball was boxed and had been in storage since the early 1980's, brought out only in 2014 with the LA84 Foundation's plan to auction it.

Cumberland beats Auburn

While Georgia Tech continued to make strides in football after 1916, Cumberland turned its attention to baseball.

Competing in the NAIA since 1984, Cumberland baseball has been a dominant force under the leadership of Coach Woody Hunt. Coach Hunt is one of only six NAIA coaches to register 1,500 career victories. Through the 2015 season Hunt, a member of the Tennessee Sports Hall of Fame, had posted a record of 1,451–608–5.

His teams have appeared in 12 NAIA World Series and have won national championships in 2004, 2010 and 2014 as well as runner-up finishes in 1995 and 2006.

The Bulldogs program has posted 24 seasons with 40 or more victories, while registering 50 or more wins eight times. Hunt's 2004 team set a school-record for victories with 59.

Cumberland has produced 64 NAIA All-Americans while 79 players of the legendary coach have signed professional contracts.

For several years Cumberland has scheduled games against teams from major conferences. It hasn't been unusual for the Bulldogs to be playing Vanderbilt, Kentucky, Tennessee, Auburn, teams from the Ohio Valley Conference and other majors on any given spring afternoon.

On March 5, 1986 Woody Hunt's team, while making a swing through the South played Auburn. Cumberland beat the Tigers 4–2 in the ninth inning. Bo Jackson, Auburn's superstar first round draft choice, went 0 for 3 with a walk for the day. The win over Auburn remains one of Coach Hunt's most memorable games.

Bulldogs out. Phoenix in.

Changing a tradition in 2016, Cumberland University made the bold move to rename its athletic teams the Phoenix thus eliminating the name Bulldogs.

School officials explained in making the announcement about the change that Cumberland's association with the Phoenix began during the Civil War when the school's administration building was burned by Union troops and a student etched on one of two columns that remained unharmed the word "Resurgam," a Greek phrase translated "I shall rise again."

After the fire Cumberland was rebuilt and many said it had risen from the ashes just as the mythical phoenix.

Kappa Sig tradition continues at both schools

Now, years after the game that largely was made possible by a Kappa Sigma fraternity chapter on Cumberland's campus, the fraternity remains prominent on the campuses of both Georgia Tech and Cumberland.

For a while the Kappa Sigma chapter at Cumberland was suspended, while the school was being operated as a private junior college. But once Cumberland's Board of Trust made the decision to return the school to four year university status, the Kappa Sigs and other fraternities and sororities returned to campus.

KAPPA SIGMA HONOR ROLL - Many of fame in a variety of professions from politics to sports claim membership in the Kappa Sigma fraternity.

Among those of national political prominence are 15 members of the U.S. House of Representatives; Jefferson Davis, president of the Confederate States of America, Transylvania University; 16 governors and six U.S. Senators.

The roll of Kappa Sig members who have served in the U.S. Senate includes Richard Burr, N.C., Wake Forest; Bob Dole, Kan., Washburn University; Paul Fannin, Ariz., University of Ariz.; Estes Kefauver, Tenn., University of Tenn.; John Tower, Tex., Southwestern University; and John McClellan, Ark.

Other Kappa Sigs of note who worked in political roles include John Ehrlichman, University of California, Nixon White House; David Kendall, Wabash College, Yale Law, attorney for President Bill Clinton; William Gibbs McAdoo, University of Tennessee, U.S. Treasury Secretary; and Larry Speakes, University of Mississippi, President Ronald Reagan's press secretary.

Topping the list of entertainers who joined Kappa Sig during their college days are Jimmy Buffett, University of Southern Mississippi, and Robert Redford, University of California. Others on this list include Hoagy Carmichael, University of Indiana; Richard Crenna, University of Southern California; Wink Martindale, Memphis State; Bill Anderson, University of Georgia; and David Nelson, University of Southern California.

A partial listing of business leaders inducted as Kappa Sig members includes Ted Turner, Brown University; Alan Mulally, CEO Ford Motor Co., University of Kansas; Mike Eskew, CEO UPS, Purdue; William Hewlett, Hewlett-Packard, Stanford, MIT; Willard Rockwell, Rockwell International, MIT; R.W. Lundgren, chairman Dow Chemical, University of Oregon; Jack Smith, president General Motors, University of Massachusetts; Scottie Mayfield, Mayfield Dairies, Georgia Tech; and John J. Donahoe, CEO EBay, Dartmouth and Stanford.

Kappa Sig members have made a significant contribution to the field of journalism. Among the most celebrated are Edward R. Murrow, renowned broadcast journalist, Washington State College (now university); Sam Donaldson, ABC News, University of Texas-El Paso; Steve Kroft, CBS 60 Minutes, Columbia University; and Lowell Thomas, news commentator, Valparaiso University, Denver University, Chicago-Kent Law School.

Football greats who were or are Kappa Sigs include Tommy Casanova, LSU; Dan Dierdorf, Michigan; Richie Cunningham, Louisiana Lafayette; Howard Harpster, Carnegie Tech; Ted Headricks, Miami; James Kent Hull, Miss. State; Bert Jones, LSU; Greg Landry, Univ. of Mass.; Elmer Oliphant, Purdue/West Point; Steve Owens, Okla.; Dick Schafrath, Ohio State; Brian Sipe, San Diego State; Jerry Stovall, LSU; Brian Young, Texas El Paso; John Michelosen, Pitt.; Richard Cunningham, Louisiana Lafayette; Clyde Scott, Arkansas/Navy; Jim Lindsey, Arkansas; and Jim Benton, Western Mich.

Other outstanding Kappa Sig names associated with sports include for golf from Wake Forest Jay Haas, Robert Wrenn, Curtis Strange, and Lanny Wilkes, and Peter Jacobsen from the Univ. of Oregon. Phil Hill, Univ. Southern Cal., is the only race car driver to be a Kappa Sig.

Several famous coaches are listed as Kappa Sigs including Cam Cameron, Indiana; William Alexander, Georgia Tech; Lloyd Carr, Missouri, Northern Michigan, and Michigan; Fisher DeBerry, Wofford; Lamar Hunt, SMU; Jerry Jones, Arkansas; and Norm Van Brocklin, Oregon.

Cumberland University

Cumberland University, located in Lebanon, Tennessee about 30 miles east of Nashville, was founded in 1842.

Although now a private independent university, the school was started by the Cumberland Presbyterian Church and later from 1946 to 1951 was owned by the Tennessee Baptist Convention.

In 1852 Cumberland opened a law school, which in a short time became a highly prestigious venue for the study of law. Cumberland's School of Law was the first law school west of the Appalachian Mountains.

Due to a number of financial challenges associated with the operation of the law school including a need to add faculty and expand library holdings as required by the American Bar Association in order to maintain accreditation, Cumberland was forced to sell the law school in 1962 to Samford University in Birmingham, Alabama, where it remains today. All assets of the school were sold to Samford for a mere $125,000.

Caruther's Hall housed Cumberland's School of Law

The Cumberland Administration building that was burned during the Civil War

During a period for about 25 years from 1956 to 1981, Cumberland, strapped financially at the time, reverted to a junior college offering associate degrees for students completing a two year course of study.

In 1981 the school's board of trust voted to return Cumberland to the status of a four year university where today baccalaureate and graduate degrees are offered in several fields of study. Cumberland's Jeanette C. Rudy School of Nursing is regarded as one of Tennessee's premier nursing schools.

Distinguished Cumberland alumni include more than 50 college and university presidents; 66 U.S. congressional leaders; 11 state governors; scores of state and federal court judges; two U.S. ambassadors; two justices of the U.S. Supreme Court; and U.S. Secretary of State Cordell Hull, father of the United Nations.

Dr. Paul C. Stumb, IV, is president of Cumberland University. The fully accredited university has an enrollment of about 1,500 students.

Georgia Institute of Technology

Founded in 1885 as the Georgia School of Technology, the Georgia Institute of Technology, known better as Georgia Tech, is a renowned public university located in downtown Atlanta with campuses in Savannah, Georgia; Metz, France; Athlone, Ireland; Shanghai, China; and Singapore.

The school's only degree program for some 16 years after its beginning was in mechanical engineering, but in 1901 the curriculum was expanded to include electrical, civil, and chemical engineering.

Currently there are six colleges within the university offering degrees in engineering, computing, business administration, the sciences, architecture, and liberal arts.

George P. (Bud) Peterson is president of Georgia Tech. The school has an endowment of approximately $1.9 billion and as recently as 2015 had an enrollment of just more than 25,000 students. The main campus in Atlanta stretches across about 375 acres.

Notable alumni include President Jimmy Carter, entertainer Jeff Foxworthy,

Ramblin' Wreck

Coca Cola chairman and CEO John F. Brock, former Atlanta mayor Ivan Allen Jr., U.S. Sen. Sam Nunn, college football coach Bill Curry, film and television actor Pernell Roberts, film actor Randolph Scott and dozens of high profile professional athletes including golfers Bobby Jones, Stewart Cink, and David Duval; football players Calvin Johnson, Joe Hamilton, Demaryius Thomas, and Joshua Nesbitt; basketball players Chris Bosh, Mark Price, Stephon Marbury, John Salley, Dennis Scott, Iman Shumpert, Derrick Favors, Jarrett Jack, Glen Rice Jr., and Kenny Anderson; and baseball players Nomar Garciaparra, Matt Murton and Mark Teixeira.

Works consulted and other references

Phoenix Rising, Dr. G. Frank Burns

Presidents Who Have Known Me, George E. Allen

The Eisenhower Presidential Library, Abilene, Kansas

The Chicago Tribune

The Georgia Tech Alumni Association

The New York Times

Lebanon, Kim Jackson Parks

The Taylor Daily Press, Taylor, Texas

Ramblinwreck.com, Georgia Tech Athletics

New Georgia Encyclopedia

Tigernet.com, Auburn Athletics

University Archives and Records Center, University of
     Pennsylvania

Wikipedia

Dr. Rick Bell, Cumberland University

Time Magazine

Cumberland University Athletics

The Atlanta Journal-Constitution

Georgia Tech photographer Danny Karnik

Photo Credits

Chapter 1

"Dwight D. Eisenhower photo portrait" by the White House is licensed under CC BY 2.0 "George-Allen-1937" by the Harris & Ewing collection at the Library of Congress is licensed under CC BY 2.0.

"Kennedy Nixon Debate (1960)" by United Press International is licensed under CC BY 2.0 "Tip O'Neill 1978" by U.S. National Archives and Records Administration is licensed under CC BY 2.0.

"Hope with Group Meets Patton WW2" by the Library of Congress is licensed under CC BY 2.0.

"Cordell Hull, U.S. Secretary of State" by U.S. Department of State from United States is licensed under CC BY 2.0.

Chapter 2

"John Heisman" by Georgia Tech Archives and Records Management is licensed under CC BY-SA 3.0.

"1913 Chevy" at the Alfred P. Sloan Museum, Flint Michigan, photo by *Trainguy1*, created July 20, 2011 is licensed under CC BY-SA 3.0.

"Horn Springs" unknown photographer used by permission of photograph owner Dr. Rick Bell, Cumberland University.

Chapter 3

"George Allen on yacht with President Truman" photographer unknown, by U.S. National Archives is licensed under CC BY-SA 3.0.

Chapter 4

"Caruthers Hall" by permission of Cumberland University from the Cumberland University Library Archives.

"Kenneth G. Matheson" source Georgia Tech Library Archives www.library.gatech.edu/archives/years/images/1906.jpg licensed under CC BY-SA 3.0.

"Gen. A.P. Stewart" photographer unknown from web.archive.org/web/20080118092045/www.generalsandbrevets.com/sgs/stewart.htm, licensed under CC BY-SA 3.0.

Chapter 5

"Heisman Trophy" source Rashaan Salaam is licensed under CC BY-SA 2.5.

Chapter 6

"Hermitage Hotel" photo by Adam Jones, used by permission as instructed by the photographer at www.flickr.com/photos/adam_jones/10234071866.

"Gentry Dugat" by permission of Cumberland University from the Cumberland University Library Archives.

Chapter 7

"Cumberland Memorial Hall" by permission of Cumberland University from the Cumberland University Library Archives.

Chapter 8

"Atlanta Georgian Terrace Hotel" Jeff Clemmons photographer from Carsonmc @ English Wikipedia is licensed under CC BY-SA 3.0.

Chapter 9

"Bayer Aspirin Bottle" source archives of Bayer AG is licensed under CC BY-SA 3.0 Unport, 2.5 Generic, 2.0 Generic and 1.0 Generic.

"Grant Field" source *www.library.gatech.edu/beck/GP575.gif* licensed under CC BY-SA 3.0.

"Grantland Rice" source the estate of Fred Russell bequeathed this picture to Jim Harwell. The file is licensed under CC BY-SA 2.5 license.

"Froggie Morrison" source Georgia Tech Library Archives, author unknown, in public domain.

"Tech's 1916 Team" source Georgia Tech History Digital Portal is licensed under CC BY-SA 3.0.

Chapter 10

"Everett (Strup) Strupper" source Georgia Tech Archives, author unknown, in public domain.

"Game Day Photo" retrieved from the Archives of both the Georgia Tech and Cumberland University athletic departments in public domain.

"Tech players tackle Cumberland running back" found at www2.cumberland.edu, author unknown, is licensed under the Creative Commons Attribution-ShareAlike.

"Walter G. (Six) Carpenter" source Georgia Tech Archives, author unknown, in public domain.

"Tech kicker Bill Fincher" source Georgia Tech Archives published in 1918 Georgia Tech's Blue Print, author unknown, in public domain.

"Tech's Joe Guyon" source Georgia Tech Library Archives, George Griffin Photograph Collection, in public domain.

Chapter 11

"Dow Cope" source Cumberland University Library Archives, photographer unknown, in public domain.

"Scoreboard" source Cumberland University Library Archives and Georgia Tech Archives, photographer unknown, in public domain.

Chapter 15

"Tech 1917 championship team" photographer Tracy Matheson and Walter Winn, The New York Times, in public domain, other versions 1917GaTechTeampic.png.

Addendum

"Tech Tower" Georgia Institute of Technology - photo taken 09/05/04 by J. Glover (AUtiger) is licensed under the *Creative Commons Attribution-Share Alike 2.5 Generic* license.

ADDENDUM

"Ramblin'Wreck" is licensed under the *Creative Commons Attribution-Share Alike 2.5 Generic* license, photographer is John Bird, 2006, originally from *en.wikipedia* and released to public domain by photographer.

"Caruthers Hall" source Cumberland University Library Archives, photographer unknown, in public domain.

"*Administration building burned during Civil War*" source Cumberland University Library Archives, photographer unknown, in public domain.

CPSIA information can be obtained at www.ICGtesting.com
Printed in the USA
LVOW11s1222170716

496553LV00003B/3/P